Riders in the Chariot

Patrick White

RIDERS

IN THE

CHARIOT

1961

The Viking Press

NEW YORK

First published in 1961 by The Viking Press, Inc.
625 Madison Avenue, New York 22, N.Y.

Published simultaneously in Canada by
The Macmillan Company of Canada Limited

Library of Congress catalog card number: 61-13728

Printed in the U.S.A. by The Colonial Press

For

Klari Daniel

and

Ben Huebsch

The Prophets Isaiah and Ezekiel dined with me, and I asked them how they dared so roundly to assert that God spoke to them; and whether they did not think at the time that they would be misunderstood, & so be the cause of imposition.

Isaiah answer'd: "I saw no God, nor heard any, in a finite organical perception; but my senses discover'd the infinite in everything, and as I was then perswaded, & remain confirm'd, that the voice of honest indignation is the voice of God, I cared not for consequences, but wrote. . . ."

I then asked Ezekiel why he eat dung, & lay so long on his right & left side? he answer'd, "The desire of raising other men into a perception of the infinite: this the North American tribes practise, & is he honest who resists his genius or conscience only for the sake of present ease or gratification?"

—WILLIAM BLAKE

Riders in the Chariot

PART ONE

Chapter 1

W HO WAS that woman?" asked Mrs. Colquhoun, a rich lady
who had come recently to live at Sarsaparilla.

"Ah," Mrs Sugden said, and laughed, "that was Miss Hare."

"She appears an unusual sort of person." Mrs Colquhoun ventured to hope.

"Well," replied Mrs Sugden, "I cannot deny that Miss Hare is
different."

But the postmistress would not add to that. She started poking at
a dry sponge. Even at her most communicative, talking with authority of the weather, which was her subject, she favoured the objective
approach.

Mrs Colquhoun was able to see for herself that Miss Hare was a
small, freckled thing, whose stockings, at that moment, could have
been coming down. To tell the truth, Mrs Colquhoun was somewhat
put out by the postmistress's discretion, but could not remain so indefinitely, for the war was over, and the peace had not yet set
hard.

Miss Hare continued to walk away from the post office, through
a smell of moist nettles, under the pale disc of the sun. An early
pearliness of light, a lamb's-wool of morning promised the millen-
nium, yet, between the road and the shed in which the Godbolds
lived, the burnt-out blackberry bushes, lolling and waiting in rusty
coils, suggested that the enemy might not have withdrawn. As Miss
Hare passed, several barbs of several strands attached themselves
to the folds of her skirt, pulling on it, tight, tight, tighter, until she
was all spread out behind, part woman, part umbrella.

"You could get torn," Mrs Godbold warned, who had come up to

3

the edge of the road, in search of something, whether child, goat, or perhaps just the daily paper.

"Oh, I could get torn," Miss Hare answered. "But what is a little tear?"

It did not matter.

Mrs Godbold was rather large. She smiled at the ground, incredulous, but glad.

"I saw a wombat," Miss Hare called.

"Not a wombat! In these parts? I do not believe you!" Mrs Godbold answered back.

Miss Hare laughed.

"What did it look like?" Mrs Godbold called, and laughed.

Still looking in the grass.

"I will tell you," Miss Hare declared, laughing, but always walking away.

It did not matter to either that much would remain unexplained. It did not matter that neither had looked at the other's face, for each was aware that the moment could yield no more than they already knew. Somewhere in the past, that particular relationship had been fully ratified.

Miss Hare went on, together with her emancipated skirt. With the back of her hand she hit a fence-post, to hear her father's bloodstone ring. She would knock thus on objects, to punctuate periods which, otherwise, might never have had an end. Now she heard the redeeming knock. She heard the wings of a bird suddenly break free from silence. She sang a little, or made sounds. All along the road—or track, the older people still called it—which rambled down from Sarsaparilla to Xanadu, the earth was black and oozy in the early morning of early spring. In all that dreamy landscape it seemed that each particle, not least Miss Hare herself, contributed towards some perfection. Nothing could be added to improve the whole.

Yet, was she not about to attempt?

Miss Hare stood still in the middle of the road. So she had stood in the post office, only, then, she had worn the kind of expression people expected.

"This is something of an occasion, Mrs Sugden," she had said.

There were those who could never understand Miss Hare's manner of speech, but the postmistress had grown used to it.

"Well, now," Mrs Sugden said, arranging some papers nicely, and the little glue bottle which use had almost glued up.

Then she waited.

"Yes," said Miss Hare.

She could not find the horrid pen. She could not find the telegraph forms, sandy like her own skin.

"I have been in touch with a person. A widow. In Melbourne. In an advertisement," she said, and found the forms. "I am engaging a housekeeper for Xanadu."

"Well, now, I am real pleased!" said Mrs Sugden, and was truly.

"You will not tell?" asked Miss Hare.

How she hated the vicious pen.

"Oh dear, no!" protested Mrs Sugden. "What is an official position if not a position of trust?"

Miss Hare considered. The post-office pen pricked the paper.

"I will tell you all about it," she decided. "But must write the telegram. To Melbourne."

Mrs Sugden knew how to wait.

Miss Hare began to write.

"She describes herself as a lady—capable and refined."

"Oh dear, I should hope so!" exclaimed Mrs. Sugden, blushing for other possibilities. "In these days, and under the same roof!"

Miss Hare ploughed her way through the ugly desert of the telegraph form.

"I am not afraid," she said. "Of anything. Or not of the things people are afraid of."

"There are other things, of course," agreed Mrs Sugden, who, in her official position, must have experienced an awful lot.

The postmistress waited. Miss Hare had on that old hat, wicker rather than straw—it was so very coarse—which she wore summer and winter regardless, and which gave her at times the look of a sunflower, at others, just an old basket coming to pieces. From where they were standing at the counter Mrs Sugden was able to look down at the kind of navel right at the centre of the crown. Miss Hare was that short. All was hat, and a hand extended from it, having trouble with a pen. The pen appeared to be resisting. Mrs Sugden stood and wondered where the hat could have come from. Nobody remembered seeing any other.

"It is all due to my Cousin Eustace Cleugh," began Miss Hare, who had just managed the signature. "He came here very many years ago. You will not remember. The way people sometimes used to send their sons on a visit to relatives in Australia. It seemed astonishing then. To *Australia!* Two wars have made a difference, of course, and the food parcels. But my Cousin Eustace came—he was somehow on my mother's side, through Aunt Fanny of Banjo Downs. Oh, it was splendid! The bachelors' quarters full. And they lit the chandelier almost every night. And balls, with music from Sydney. My mother said I should mingle with the guests—I was then a young girl; my hair had just been put up—but how could I mingle when I must watch all the people who had come to Xanadu? There was one girl—I must tell you—called Helen Antill, in a dress embroidered with tiny mirrors. I overheard my mother remark that perhaps she should not have invited that Miss Antill. 'Nor any other girl,' my father replied; 'nor young men either.' My father had to have his joke. 'And let us enjoy our pudding in peace,' he said, 'and bread sauce.' My father was fond of bread sauce with a roast fowl, and one of the cooks used to make him a special kind."

"Ah?"

"With *crushed onion!*" cried Miss Hare.

Mrs Sugden shifted foot. Much of her life had been spent in waiting.

"But let me see—my Cousin Eustace, who came and went, was in some way disappointing to my parents, though in after years he made amends. Oh dear, yes, he made me a little allowance, because his circumstances permitted, from the island of Jersey where he lives. That began already during my mother's lifetime. Fortunately. Because something—I never understood what—happened to my father's business."

Miss Hare's voice trailed off. She took up the second, and equally horrid post-office pen. But her gesture remained an irrelevant one.

"What do you know!" said Mrs Sugden.

"Oh, yes," sighed Miss Hare. "I thought *you* knew. I had been receiving the allowance so many years. Till suddenly the island of Jersey was overrun. Like that."

Miss Hare did, in fact, spill the remaining post-office ink, but Mrs Sugden appeared not to care.

"By Germans?"

"Who else?" replied Miss Hare, not without contempt. "Like darkness. For years there was no communication from our relative, until on a Friday morning, exactly seven weeks ago, a few lines arrived to say my Cousin Eustace was safe. Although in only moderate health and reduced circumstances, he considered it his duty to continue rendering me some small assistance."

Mrs Sugden was suitably rejoiced at such a lifting of the clouds.

"And so you were able to engage this lady."

"This woman has almost agreed."

Miss Hare could be at moments both realistic and stern.

"Her name is Mrs Jolley," she added, and, as the extent of the morning struck her through the window: "I do hope she is capable of being happy at Xanadu. Sydney is not Melbourne, and here on the outskirts, there is such a lot of grass."

"Anybody can be happy if they have a mind to be," offered the postmistress, regardless of whether her maxim was cut to fit the situation.

Some flies had died on the counter which separated the two women, who found themselves examining the bodies.

"What," asked Mrs Sugden, taking a deep breath, "what became of the girl called Helen Antill, who wore that lovely dress?"

"Oh, she went away," said Miss Hare. "Everybody goes away."

She began to swing her right leg. Her face, which narrative had turned moist and crumbly, was become dry and stale again. Ordinarily when she spoke, her mouth stayed stiff, almost as if she had had a stroke.

"She went away, and married, but somebody we had never heard of, and lived in a house, and had children, and buried her husband. Once I saw her looking out of the window at something."

Mrs Sugden looked away, as if she, too, had seen.

Just then there was a crunching, and a person approached—it was, in fact, the newcomer to Sarsaparilla, Mrs Colquhoun—with the result that Miss Hare let the present fall like a shutter.

"Thank you," she said to Mrs Sugden, whom she could have met only the moment before, and left.

So there was Miss Hare, on the track which the Council had begun to call a road, sometimes even avenue, which led down from Sarsaparilla to Xanadu. At one point doubts had invested her, and turned her stony still, but uncertain prospects could not long resist the surge of her surroundings, and she soon went on. Where the road sloped down she ran, disturbing stones, her body quite agitated as it accompanied her, but her inner self by now joyfully serene. The anomaly of that relationship never failed to mystify, and she stopped again, to consider. For a variety of reasons, very little of her secret, actual nature had been disclosed to other human beings. She stood still. Thinking very intently. Or allowing her instincts to play around her. Although no other human being was actually present, she did resent what must eventually recur. She stroked leaves sulkily. She broke a shaggy stick. Other people would drive along a bush road looking out of the windows of a car, but their minds embraced almost nothing of what their flickering eyes saw. Whole towers of green remained unclimbed, rocks unopened. Or else the intruders might stop their cars, and go in search of water. She had seen them, letting themselves down into the cold, black, secret rock pools, while remaining enclosed in their own resentful goose-flesh. Whereas she, Miss Hare, whose eyes were always probing, fingers trying, would achieve the ecstasy of complete, annihilating liberation without any such immersion.

Now, for a moment, she looked angry.

But drifted on dreamily.

All that land, stick and stone, belonged to her, over and above actual rights. Nobody else had ever known how to penetrate it quite to the same extent. She went on through her peculiar territory, lolloping, stopping. Often stopping. The sky had quickened, and was now a lively blue. The rather scrubby, indigenous trees, not so much of interest to the eye as an accompaniment to states of mind, were at the moment behaving with docility, a certain, languid melancholy. Until she arrived at the bottom, where the road turned, and curled, and rose. The slope, gentle at first, climbed to abrupter terraces, with dispensations of fern and moss, and soft, rotting carpets, and there the trees, it seemed, grew straighter, taller, and invariably she would turn dizzy if she stared too long upward at their scintillating crowns.

The owner never approached her legal property by following the official road to the gates—those, with their attempt at heraldry, were chained and padlocked, anyway—but took a short cut that she and the Godbold children always used, or an even shorter one, as now, known only to herself, and along which she had to push and struggle, actually to tunnel. But the way developed over good, soft loam, and velvet patches of leaf mould, lovely if the knees were allowed to sink for a moment into a surface from which would rise the scent of fungus and future growth.

So Miss Hare was pushing and struggling now, because it was what she liked, and chose. Scratched a little, but that was to be expected once the feet were set upon the paths of existence. Slapped by a staggy elder-bush, of which the buds had almost reached the edible stage. Whipped by the little sarsaparilla vine, of which she could have drunk the purple up. Stroked by ferns, and ferns.

At one stage she fell upon the knees of her earth-coloured, practical stockings, not because she was discouraged, or ill—she had reached the time of life where acquaintances and neighbours were always on the lookout for strokes—but because it was natural to adopt a kneeling position in the act of worship, and because intense conviction will sometimes best express itself through the ungainliness of spontaneity.

So she rested a little upon her knees, under the great targe of her protective hat, and dug her blunt, freckled fingers into the receptive earth. She knelt for a while in the tunnel that led to Xanadu, and anybody would have found her more grotesquely ugly, less acceptable than they had thought. If family had remained to her, other than her Cousin Eustace, who was at a distance, and a handful of Urquhart Smiths, who had decided to forget, they would have turned away on recognizing such a travesty of their otherwise irreproachable strain.

In the past the Hares had always blamed the Urquhart Smiths, and the Urquhart Smiths, with equal determination, had blamed the Hares. But now there were not many of either to argue and discuss. If it had not been for Norbert Hare himself one might have expected normality from such an untainted, bourgeois stock, for Norbert was the son of old Mr Hare, the wine merchant at Wynyard, as everybody knew. The Urquhart Smiths, understandably, knew it better than anybody else, and, forgetting the Smiths in favour of the Urquharts, were always ready to remind their Eleanor who had married Norbert.

Eleanor was of that branch of the family at Mumblejug, of whom Sir Dudley, it will be remembered, arrived in New South Wales during the last century to represent the Queen. Renowned for his silk hats and horsemanship, Sir Dudley was an exemplary man, as his descendants had continued to tell long after everybody else had forgotten. If his daughter Eleanor was less remindful than some of the collaterals, it was perhaps because of her discreet temper, her indifferent health, and certainly, her unorthodox marriage. Of four sisters, she was the only one to survive. All lovely, gracious girls, three were buried before they had been matched, under the gum trees, outside the little Gothic church which Sir Dudley had built at Mumblejug, not so much to exalt the spirit, as to perpetuate a materialist tradition.

So solid, so lovely-old, so *English,* Sir Dudley's church seemed to proclaim the situation at Mumblejug as indestructible. And then Eleanor went and did that terrible thing, of marrying Norbert, the son of old Hare the wine merchant at Wynyard. People of account, quite unacquainted with the Urquhart Smiths, were shocked into sympathy with them. Eleanor, however, departed with her portion, and many lesser individuals laughed.

It was not that anybody failed to respect old Mr Hare. Nobody suspected his fortune of being anything less than considerable; nor were the matrimonial expectations of nice people particularly sanguine in such a recent society, unless the arrival of some Honourable roused intemperate hopes. All considered, a girl might have done worse than catch a Hare, and if practical minds did not quickly and quietly accept Eleanor Urquhart Smith's choice, the fault lay with her husband. Who was original.

Norbert Hare had never been given to half-measures. He did, or contemplated doing, things which nobody else would have thought of. He once rode a grey horse up the marble stairs at Xanadu, as far as the landing, it was said, where his mount took fright, and deposited a mound of glaring yellow on the runner. Although they were not always executed, Norbert was forever conceiving plans: for building a study at the top of a Chinese pagoda, or stable in the shape of a mosque, for breeding *escargots de Bourgogne,* or planting medlars, or printing poems—his own—on sheets of coloured silk, woven for that purpose on the property. The wine merchant's son had received an education which his own peculiar temperament ensured was of a spasmodic and eclectic kind. At one period he had considered writing a treatise on Catullus, until discovering he was out of patience with that poet. Norbert had, in fact, written quantities himself: epigrams, and metaphysical fragments, which he would read aloud to anybody he succeeded in cornering. The fragment, it appeared, possessed for him a greater distinction than the whole.

There were all those pieces of marble he brought from Italy. He brought the mosaics for a bath, all nymphs, and vines, and a big, black, baleful goat. Two Italian artisans were imported purposely to fit the pieces together, after it had been promised they would receive a regular supply of *vino*. The Italians came and practised their art, and drank their wine, and one of them, it was never decided which, got an Irish girl with child. Norbert and Eleanor were absent a good deal, of course, in foreign parts, because it was the period when Australians of That Class—and Norbert was soon of That Class—were returning Home to show they were as good as anyone else. So the Hares had to go, nor could the discreet Eleanor prevent rumours trickling back: that Norbert had been involved in a duel while passing through Perugia, and that in London he had fallen down in public while under the influence of strong drink. It was all in character. But Norbert's grandest gesture, the one that caused people to suck their teeth, to gnash them, or to set them in a kind, sad smile, was the building of his folly at Sarsaparilla outside Sydney. His Pleasure Dome, he called it, his Xanadu, and recited the appropriate verses to lady guests as they strolled in their veils and the afternoon, inspecting the freshly laid foundations of porous yellow stone.

Nothing exquisite can be created in a hurry, and Xanadu was no exception. It cost time and patience; everybody grew exhausted. But there it stood finally: golden, golden, in a frill or two of iron lace, beneath the dove-grey thatching of imported slates, its stables and bachelor quarters trailing out behind. So Norbert, son of old Mr Hare, the wine merchant at Wynyard, was vindicated at last, if only in his own sight. He liked to climb up through his house, and on reaching the top, with its little, actual dome of faintly amethyst glass, spend a private hour devouring the flesh of a cold fowl, skimming opening lines from obscure poets, or just staring out over his own property. Or beyond, it could have been—beyond the still manageable park which he had ordered to be planted, beyond even the grey, raggedy native scrub, for his eyes appeared momentarily appeased, and that end might not have been achieved, if anchorage in time and space had forced him to recognize the native cynicism of that same grey, raggedy scrub.

The scrub, which had been pushed back, immediately began to tangle with Norbert Hare's wilfully created park, until, years later, there was his daughter, kneeling in a tunnel of twigs which led to Xanadu. Speckled and dappled, like any wild thing native to the place, she was examining her surroundings for details of interest. Almost all were, because alive, changing, growing, personal, like her own thoughts, which intermingled, flapping and flashing, with the leaves, or lay straight and stiff as sticks, or emerged with the painful stench of any crushed ant. Her hands, almost always dirty and scratched, from the constant need to plunge into operations of importance: encouraging a choked plant to shoot, freeing a fledgling from its shell, breaking an afterbirth, were now hung with dying ants, she observed with some distress. One slithered from her father's bloodstone ring, which she wore not as a memento of her father, but because its device officially confirmed her ownership of Xanadu.

Once or twice in the far past she had attempted to play with the ring on her father's hand.

"It is not a toy," he had warned. "You must learn to respect property."

So she had begun to.

The mother, also, had worn rings, amethysts for preference. She favoured the twilight colours. Her clothes were in no way memorable, except perhaps her collection of woolly wraps, of such lightness they could not possibly have weighed upon her. The little girl was allowed to touch the clothes and rings her mother wore, even to grow rough with them. Too delicate to protest much, unless an issue exceeded the bounds of taste, Eleanor Hare wished most earnestly to do what was right, as wife and mother.

"I am so afraid, Norbert, we shall not love our child enough. With my health. And your interests."

"Oh, *love!*" the father replied, and laughed fit to shatter it forever.

"I had no intention of causing you pain," his wife complained, before withdrawing into herself, under a big woolly shawl, a sagegreen, and a hot-water bottle which she would hold to her neuralgia.

"If only you would prevent her knocking over coffee cups," he requested, "especially into the laps of guests, and snapping off dahlias, and stamping up and down the landing while I am reading. I need a certain amount of silence while I am thinking something out."

"It is only reasonable," she agreed, "that a child should learn to respect other people's needs."

Anybody's reasonableness, and particularly his wife's, was what infuriated him most.

So the child learned, as far as her natural clumsiness would allow, to move softly, like a leaf, and certain words she avoided, because they were breakable. The word LOVE, for instance, brittle as glass, and far more precious. Oh, she could go carefully enough in the end, in little, starched movements. And had learnt to love, even, but after her secret fashion, the labyrinths of corridors, the big, cool, greenish rooms, the golden walls of stone, the tunnels through the shrubberies.

And now Miss Hare got up, as far as her tunnel would allow, to continue struggling, bundling, pushing with the shield of her great wicker hat, to burst forth, not without shaking, and panting, and ridiculousness, into the presence of her noble love.

On extricating herself from the embrace of twigs, there remained perhaps another two hundred yards of less grudgingly gracious green: a pomegranate almost gone to wood, a crab or two, spidery with first blossom, several sad, but soothing pines. The ground continued to rise, increasing her breathlessness, tearing her calves open as she climbed. All, whether within or without, was leading upward now.

So Miss Hare came home, as always, for the first time. She stepped out beyond the trees where lawn began. Certainly the grass appeared a bit neglected, but the eyes, and not necessarily the eyes of a lover, were invariably transfixed by their first glimpse of Xanadu. Miss Hare herself had almost crumbled as she stood to watch her vision form.

❧✣❧

Chapter 2

S HE LIKED to come downstairs early. She would even get up in the dark, bumping things before she found her balance. She liked to come down, and sit, and listen to the house, after her own footsteps had died away, and the sound of the primus on which she had brewed a pot of tea. Then, she would sit and wrinkle her nose at the smell of kerosene, while she thawed out, if it were winter, or relaxed in summer after the weight of the heavy nights. Later she would start to walk about, touching things. Sometimes she would move them: a goblet, or a footstool, and once a heavy buhl table, from which the brass had risen to set traps for clothes and flesh. But mostly she let things lie, out of respect. Or she would draw a curtain, cunningly, to look out at the spectacle of morning, when all that is most dense becomes most transparent, and the world is dependent on the eye of the beholder. Then Miss Hare's mouth would grow slack and loving as she formed the solid trunks of gums out of the grey embryos of trees.

She was at her best early in the morning. Except on this one. She jerked the curtain. And it tore, uglily. A long tongue of gold brocade. But she did not stay to consider. It was several mornings since she had taken the postmistress into her confidence. It was the morning before the arrival of the housekeeper at Xanadu.

"A housekeeper!" she said, feeling her knuckles to test their infirmity, and finding they were, indeed, infirm.

A housekeeper, though, was less formidable than a person, and this was what Miss Hare dreaded most: an individual called Mrs Jolley, whose hips would assert themselves in navy blue, whose breathing would be heard, whose letters would lie upon the furniture

14

addressed in the handwriting of daughters and nieces, telling of lives lived, unbelievably, in other places. It was frightening, frightening.

Miss Hare often cried in private, not from grief, but because she found it soothing, and she did now. It was frightening, though. Naturally she found it impossible to like human beings, if only on account of their faces, to say nothing of their habit of relating things that had never happened and then believing that they had. Children were perhaps the worst, because they had not yet grown insincere, and insincerity does blunt the weapons of attack. Possible exceptions were those children who grew up in one's vicinity, almost without one's noticing, just being around; that was delicious, like air. Best of all Miss Hare liked those who never expected what they would not receive. She liked animals, birds, and plants. On these she would expend her great, but pitiable love, and because that was not expected, it ceased to be pitiable.

Once, it was related, a naked nestling had fallen into her lap, and she had reared it by some mysterious method of her own, warming it down her front, it was suspected, and ejecting juices into its beak from her mouth. The nestling had grown into a dove. Some of the Godbold children had been shown it. Then it flew away, of course, but would return sometimes, Miss Hare told. She would talk to it. Everybody except the Godbold kids thought it a lot of rot, Miss Hare talking to birds. But you could learn, she insisted. Miss Hare said you could learn to do anything, provided you wanted to, but there were an awful lot of things you did not want enough.

Like learning to love a human being. Like the housekeeper, whom the telegram and her own increasing infirmity were bringing to Xanadu.

"Ah, no, no, no!" she protested and whimpered in the cold, early-morning air.

And the house repeated it after her.

Most of those landowners who wished to show how rich they were had already gone on to build in brick at the time when Norbert Hare decided to cut his dash in stone. To Mr Hare, brick was plain ugly; it did not please him a little bit, and what was Xanadu to suggest, if not the materialization of beauty, and climax of his pleasure? *Pleasure* is a shocking word in societies where the most luxurious aspirations are disguised as humble, moral ones. It is doubtful whether any rich, landowning gentleman of the period would have admitted to his house's being more than *necessary* or *practical*. Material objects were valued for their *usefulness;* if they were also intended to *please,* not to say *glorify,* it was commonly kept a secret. Only Norbert Hare, notoriously rash, had been heard to confess that the word *useful* sounded to him less modest than humiliating. It was so intolerably grey and Australian. *Brilliant* and *elegant* were the epithets applicable to Norbert's aspirations, certainly to his most ambitious, his Pleasure Dome at Xanadu. Although by no means a sincere man, there was one point in his life at which sincerity conferred with taste and individualism. Xanadu was Norbert's contribution to the sum of truth, *brilliant* and *elegant* though the house was, created in the first place for its owner's *pleasure.* More would have admired it openly, if they could have felt the principles of their admiration to be sound. As it was, other monied gentlemen voiced more loudly than ever their enthusiasm for the *practical* qualities of brick, and were persuaded that if the turrets of their purple mansions conformed to the pattern then condoned, nobody was going to accuse simple, down-to-earth sheepkeepers of acting in any way *flash.*

Norbert, of course, did not keep sheep; his family might have laughed a little longer if he had. What he possessed was the fortune of his wine-merchant father, who died conveniently soon after his son's marriage, followed by several commercial brothers, trustful to the point of overlooking brilliance in a nephew. Norbert Hare inherited all, and thus comfortably endowed, set about leading the life of a country gentleman, such as he understood it from his reading and his travels, with none of the colonial encumbrances of sheep and acres which made the undertaking virtually impossible. What he required, and did, in fact, acquire, was an exquisite setting for his humours: the park of exotic, deciduous trees, the rose garden which his senses craved, pasture for the pedigree Jersey cows which would fill his silver jugs with cream, and stables for the horses which he drove himself with virtuosity—always greys, always four-in-hand. Thus surrounded and provided for, he was soon engrossed in living up to it all: advising on the drenching of a cow, or blistering of a horse (Mr Hare always knew), marshalling the cinerarias in extra brilliant ranks, interfering in his daughter's education, tearing down a wall, throwing out a wing, or running upstairs to jot down some thought which had occurred invariably to someone else before him.

Despite the inevitable frustrations and migraines, life at Xanadu was never squalid. Out of its bower of rather unhappy exotic trees, out of its necklaces of rosebeds (the complexions of the blooms themselves protected by little parasols, which occupied practically the whole of the second gardener's time) aspired the lovely languid house. Round it they had trained wistaria, which at the height of the Hares' glory had not attained to vulgar opulence, and which never failed to please the eye in the same way as a feather boa on the right neck. In the spring its heavy, clovy scent invaded the great, greenish rooms; the marble staircase and the malachite urns dissolved beneath the onslaught, and the gilded mirrors led by subtle, receding stages far beyond the bounds of vision.

The beauty of it antagonized some of those whom the Hares were in the habit of regarding as friends, to say nothing of the practical relatives, Ted Urquhart Smith, for instance, one of the cousins from Banjo Downs.

"What becomes of all this flummery when Bert has blown the cash?" asked Ted on one occasion, indicating with calloused hand the drawing-room at Xanadu, in which it was almost impossible to tell where glass ended and light began.

Addie, his sister, permitted herself a titter.

His Cousin Eleanor hesitated. Grave even as a girl, life with her husband had made her graver still.

"But I think Norbert's fortune is very prudently invested," she replied at last. "And then, a house is said to be an investment in itself."

The wife of Norbert Hare seldom committed herself to positive opinions. Two positives in that relationship would have been intolerable.

Once, in a fit of rage, the husband accused his wife of having become the mouthpiece of social cliché.

"But it is what people prefer, Norbert," the poor woman protested, with vehemence for her. "Too much of what is unexpected is too upsetting."

Before there was any call for it she began to wear, together with her apologetic amethysts, colours which suggested mourning. She would cough thinly, from behind an expression that invited inquiry into the state of her health, and visitors would take the hint, not that they really cared to discover how Mrs Hare's health was poor, but it provided a useful topic with which to hack a way into the tangles of conversation.

She was not a snob, though there were many who accused her of it. She suffered, rather, from seeing the weak exposed to those whom she considered strong, and so, she would attempt to keep her friends separate, in compartments that she hoped might protect them from one another. She was completely unreal, and would impart temporarily to those of her equals with whom she came in contact something of her unreality. Yet she was not ineffective against the peacock colours of the stage at Xanadu, and provided the perfect, flat foil to her husband's fustian. The one cataclysmic reality to challenge her playing of the part was the presence of her daughter, but that was a fact she had failed from the beginning to embrace, an event the significance of which she had recoiled from relating to the play of life.

After several years of tedious and frustrated childbirth, Mrs Hare had succeeded in having this little girl. They named her Mary, because the mother, fortunately, was too exhausted to think, and the father, who would have plunged with voluptuous excitement into the classics, or the works of Tennyson, to dredge up some shining name for a son, turned his back on the prospect of a daughter. So, Mary the latter became, but an innocent, Protestant one.

Mrs Hare had soon taken refuge from Mary in a rational kindness, with which she continued to deal her a series of savage blows during what passed for childhood.

"My darling must decide how best she can repay her parents for all she owes them," was amongst the mother's favourite tactics. "See all these beautiful things they have put here to be enjoyed, not smashed in thoughtless games."

And, in answer to a frequent question: "Only our Father in Heaven will be able to tell my pet why He made her as He did."

Paddling in her own delicious shallows, it never occurred to Mrs Hare to raise her eyes to God, except to call Him as a formal witness. She accepted Him—who would have been so audacious not to?—but as the creator of a moral and a social system. At that level, she could always be relied on to put her hand in her purse, to help repair vestments, or support fallen girls, and her name was published for everyone to read, on a visiting card, inserted in a brass frame, on the end of her regular pew.

The little girl appeared gravely to accept the attitudes adopted by her mother, but was not genuinely influenced. Unattached, she drifted through the pale waters of her mother's kindness like a little, wondering, transparent fish, in search of those depths which her instinct told her could exist.

Her father's attitudes were less acceptable than her mother's.

Once in her presence—or she had been standing, rather, in the drawing-room alcove, apart, touching the waves of an emerald silk with which the day-bed would fascinate the fingers—her father had thrown down his cap with more than his usual violence, and shouted, "Who would ever have thought I should get a *red* girl! By George, Eleanor, she is ugly, ugly!"

Which—it sounded—was the worst that might be said.

With more than her usual kindness, Eleanor Hare motioned to their child, and when the latter had come forward—because what else could anyone do?—the mother smoothed a sash, and sighed, and suggested, "Plain is the word, Norbert. And who knows—Mary's plainness may have been given to her for a special purpose."

Because she was inexperienced, or because she was born hopeful, Mary did not immediately begin to hate her father. She decided on a watery smile, which only made her uglier, and her parent more enraged.

She remained altogether without companions, because it never occurred to anybody that she was in need of them, and she did fairly well without: with sticks, pebbles, skeleton leaves, birds, insects, the hollows of trees, and the cellars and attics of Xanadu. She did have a pony, but preferred to be with it rather than to ride upon it—which would have entailed the company of her father—and soon learned to oblige most of its wishes by studying the quiver of a nostril, the flicker of a muscle, and the varying assertions of silence.

Once when, unavoidably, in the company of her father, and they had gone down to inspect a rested paddock, she had thrown herself on the ground, and begun to hollow out a nest in the grass, with little feverish jerks of her body, and foolish grunts, curling round in the shape of a bean, or position of a foetus. So it appeared to him. But, in answer to his quick-drawn demand for an explanation, the child had replied, simply, "Now I know what it feels like to be a dog."

He had been so shocked and disgusted by the expression on her freckled face, that he told her to get up at once, and decided not to think about the incident again.

On very few occasions Mary Hare and her father, approaching from their opposite sides, arrived simultaneously at a common frontier of understanding, and then only when alcohol, despair, or approaching death loosened the slight restraints of reason—when, indeed, he came closest to resembling in her eyes a distressed or desperate animal.

Throughout her life the daughter would remember an incident which occurred about that time, and on which she would employ her intuition in attempting to interpret what her mind failed to understand. She had been standing on the terrace. It was the hour of sunset. Earlier in the afternoon they had gone driving along the roads and lanes round Sarsaparilla, even as far as Barranugli, so that her father might show himself. How relieved she felt to be alone at last, able to look at, and touch, and smell whatever she saw, without danger of being asked by her parents for explanations. The urns on the terrace were running over, she remembered, with cascades of a little milky flower, which would shimmer through darkness like falls of moonlight. But at that hour the light was gold. Or red. So splendid that even she, a red girl, had no need to feel ashamed of the correspondence.

Then her father came outside. He had been tasting a new brandy which they had sent out for his personal opinion, and his mouth was still wet and shining from his recent occupation. His eyes, in the dazzle from the sun, appeared almost vulnerable. There they stood, the father and daughter, facing each other, alarmingly exposed. He came forward, and seemed at once both puzzled and assured. Fondling her. Which was not his habit. And it was not altogether pleasant: his hands playing amongst her hair. She was reminded of a pair of black-and-white spaniels she had seen lolloping and playing together, too silly to help themselves. But just because her father's temporary silliness and loss of control had reduced him to the level of herself and dogs, she did submit to his fondling her.

She did not remember what he said, not all of it, for that, too, was silly and confused, only that at one point he had shaken his head, as if to dash the sunlight out of his eyes, both frowning and smiling, and spoke in a harsh voice, which, although addressing her, did not seem designed for her attention.

Her father said: "Who are the riders in the Chariot, eh, Mary? Who is ever going to know?"

Who, indeed? Certainly *she* would not be expected to understand. Nor did she think she wanted to, just then. But they continued there, the sunset backed up against the sky, as they stood beneath the great swingeing trace-chains of its light. Perhaps she should have been made afraid by some awfulness of the situation, but she was not. She had been translated: she was herself a fearful beam of the ruddy, champing light, reflected back at her own silly, uncertain father.

Then he had started frowning, and it became obvious they were again driving along the road from Barranugli to Sarsaparilla, returning through the comparatively humdrum light of the afternoon already past.

"I do not like the off-side front mare," he complained. "Must replace the off-side front. She moves lame, without her being lame at all."

For he required perfection in horses, as in everything, and usually got it, except in human beings.

He looked at her, and was again irritated, she saw, because she was such an ugly little girl, and she, for her part, could do nothing for him but smile back in the way of those from whom nothing much is expected.

Yet, the father's rather oblique remark, made when he was drunk, and uttered with the detachment and harshness of male egotism, encouraged the daughter to expect of life some ultimate revelation. Years after, when his stature was even further diminished in her memory, her mind would venture in foxy fashion, or more blunderingly wormlike, in search of a concealed truth. If fellowship with Himmelfarb and Mrs Godbold, and perhaps her brief communion with a certain blackfellow, would confirm rather than expound a mystery, the reason could be that, in the last light, illumination is synonymous with blinding.

In the meantime, life at Xanadu was disturbed less by transcendental problems than by the economic and social ones which come to those who enjoy nerves and invested income. The Hares never talked about money. To Mrs Hare that would have been an act in the poorest taste. To her husband, on the other hand, money was something he did not care to think about, but which he hoped fervently would still be there. He was not unlike a traveller walking into a landscape which may prove mirage. Fortunate in his inherit-

ance from the wine-merchant father and commercial uncles, and in
the devotion of an individual just stupid enough to be honest, just
intelligent enough to be practical, who managed his late father's business, Norbert was pretty certain that his landscape was an actual one.
But it unnerved him to discuss it, and if drink or insomnia forced
him to consider his financial future, he would buy reality off by writing to his London agent to order a fireplace in Parian marble, or a
Bonington, which, he was assured, would soon be coming up for
sale. In that way he was fortified.

In that way they continued to live at Xanadu, and soon it became
clear the daughter of the house was a young girl. They put up her
hair, and the nape of her neck was greenish and unfreckled where
the red hair had lain. She was no prettier, however, and unnaturally
small.

The mother began to sigh a good deal, and remarked, "It is time
we thought about doing something for our poor Mary."

But immediately wondered whether her suggestion might not
have sounded vulgar.

The father could not feel the situation deserved his interest.

"If anything is to happen, it will happen." He yawned, and
showed his rather handsome, pointed teeth. "How does it happen to
at least ninety per cent of the unlikely human race? How did it happen to us?"

"We grew fond of each other," his wife ventured, and blushed.

The husband laughed out loud.

And the wife preferred not to hear.

Not long after, Mrs Hare displayed excitement and her husband
cynical interest when it was announced that Eustace Cleugh intended to undertake a tour of the world, in the course of which he
would visit his relations in New South Wales. Except that he was a
member of an English branch of Urquhart Smiths, not a lot was
known about Mr Cleugh, but blank sheets are always whitest. Mrs
Hare *had* heard that her Cousin Eustace was *awfully nice,* neither
young, nor yet middle-aged, comfortably off, and that his mother's
brother had married the Honourable Lavinia Lethbridge, a daughter
of Lord Trumpington.

"What does Mr Cleugh do for a living?" Mary asked her mother.

"I don't exactly know," replied the latter. "I expect he just lives."

So, it all sounded most desirable.

Eustace Cleugh, when he arrived, was not surprised at a lot of what he heard and saw, for as an Englishman and an Urquhart Smith, he had preconceived notions of what he must expect from colonial life in general and the Norbert Hares in particular.

"Breeding is ninety per cent luck, whatever the experts and Urquhart Smiths may tell you," Mr Hare announced the first night at dinner. "And when I say luck, I mean bad luck, of course."

"There are so many *rewarding* topics!" his wife complained, looking at her cherry stones.

Mary Hare stared at her cousin. An absence of interested upbringing had at least left her with a thorough training in observation, and although she looked deeper than was commonly considered decent, she often made discoveries. Now she confirmed that this man was, in fact, as her mother had forewarned, neither young, nor yet middle-aged. To Mary Hare it seemed probable that Mr Cleugh had always been about thirty-five. As she herself was of indeterminate age, she hoped they might become friends. But how was she to go about it? In the first place, he was of her father's sex. In the second, his beautifully kept, slightly droopy moustache, and the long bones of his folded-fan-like hands, appeared unaware of anything beyond the person of Eustace Cleugh. Perhaps if he had been a dog—say, an elegant Italian greyhound—she might have won him over by many infallible means.

But as that was not the case, she could only offer him an almond.

Which he accepted with an unfolding of hands. Now also he began to unfold his mind, and to offer to the audience in general— everything that Eustace spoke was offered to a general, rather than to a particular, audience—an account of a journey he had made with a friend through Central and Northern Italy.

"After a short interlude at Ravenna," Mr Cleugh picked his way, "not in itself of interest, but there are the mosaics, and the *zuppa di pesce*—and they are essential, aren't they?—we went on to Padua, where the Botanic Gardens are said to be the oldest in Europe. They are not, I must admit, particularly large, or *fine,* as gardens go, but we found them to be of peculiarly subtle horticultural interest."

Mrs Hare made the little social noises that one made. But her husband had begun to blink, repeatedly, and hard.

"In Padua, poor Aubrey Puckeridge was struck down by some ailment we were never able to diagnose, part tummy, part fever, in what turned out to be—our guidebook had sadly misinformed us—a most primitive *albergo*."

Mrs Hare made the same, only slightly more appreciative noises.

"And did he die?" asked Norbert.

"Well, no," replied Eustace Cleugh. "I hope I did not imply. I intended only to suggest that poor Aubrey was awfully indisposed."

"Oh," said Mr Hare. "I thought perhaps the fellow died."

Eustace Cleugh noticed that his cousin's husband had been drinking a good deal of his own poisonous wine.

Mary Hare was fascinated by Mr Cleugh's story, not so much by the narrative as by how it issued out of his face. She put it together in piles of dead leaves, but neatly, and matched, like bank-notes. It made her sad, too. So many of the things she told died on coming to the surface, when their life, to say nothing of their after life in her mind, could be such a shining one. She wondered whether Mr Cleugh realized how dead his own words were, and if he was suffering for it. There were, after all, many things he and she had in common, if they could first overcome the strangeness of their separate existences, and crack the codes of human intercourse.

"When he got better, and left that primitive *albergo*," she asked, for a start, offering him her assistance.

But Eustace Cleugh no longer felt inclined.

He had only glanced at his cousin's ugly child, and promised himself that, during his visit, he would look as little as possible in that direction. Her short, stumpy hands were particularly repulsive, and the flare of hair that had not yet submitted to the tyranny of pins. He shuddered inside himself. Even while concentrating on the pattern of his dessert plate, he was conscious of how shockingly the girl was put together. It was almost as though the presence of any kind of physical monstrosity was a personal insult to Mr Cleugh.

"I expect Cousin Eustace is tired." Mrs Hare was making his excuses. "My own arrival in a strange house exhausts me beyond anything."

Eustace, of course, turned a smile on the company, because his manners were perfect, and became murmurous in protest.

But he did retire early, and not to the bachelors' quarters, because, said Mrs Hare, he was a member of the family.

Mary soon realized that her life would remain unchanged by their cousin's being with them, because she did not see so very much of him; he was always either reading or writing—his tastes appeared studious—smoking or thinking, or walking in the bush to study the flora of Australia.

Once she suggested, "If you like, I shall come with you. I shall take you to places that probably no one else has seen. Only, you mustn't mind crawling and scrambling. And sometimes there are snakes."

He could smile very obligingly. He said, "That is a good idea. Yes. Why have we not thought of it before? Yes. Some day. When there is more time."

Because there were also social engagements: gentlemen were brought, who told him about their sheep, and ladies, who wished to be told about Home, some mythical land that existed largely in their imaginations. A lot of this did at last surprise the visitor, for it had never occurred to him that sheep could be taken seriously, and together with his English acquaintances, he had always considered that, of all civilizations, real and imagined, only the Italian was worthy of consideration.

All the time Mrs Hare remained aware that something must be done for Mary, and so it was decided to give the ball. This was such an undertaking in itself that it did not occur to her how her daughter might be affected by it.

The latter did venture, "Do you think Cousin Eustace cares about dancing? He is far too polite to say whether he does or not."

But already, mentally, the mother was at the dressmaker's. She was calculating how many oyster patties, and wondering whether in the final hour the maids would obey her orders.

Even on the night, everyone was inclined to ignore Mary Hare. Those who were kind enough thought to respect her feelings by not noticing her appearance, but those who were cruel hoped to spare their own by refusing to see what could only upset them.

She appeared dressed in a silvery white, because she was a young girl, and this was to be the moment of her triumph, or sacrifice. She stood about, touching the papery stuff of her skirt with disbelieving hands, wearing jewels which her mother had brought from her own box: a little brooch in knots of pearls, and pearl dog-collar which the mother herself no longer wore, and which had lost much of its lustre from lying on velvet instead of on living flesh.

So there she was, dressed to kill, as one young fellow remarked, only it was Mary who was killed, by her own pearl dog-collar.

Certainly it was rather tight. She was always inclined to be red, however, in patches, according to weather and emotion, to say nothing of rough. Her hands caught in the splendid stuff of her silvery dress, and she was reminded of the many awkwardnesses of behaviour of which she had been guilty. Perhaps the most grotesque detail of her whole appearance, those who discussed it remembered afterwards, was a little bunch of ridiculous flowers that she had pinned half-wilting at her waist: frail fuchsia, and rank geranium, and pinks, and camomile—all stuffed together, and trembling, and falling. It did certainly look peculiar, and most unsuccessful, but she had not been able to resist one touch of what she knew by heart.

The evening developed, in gusts of music, and tinkling of glass. The ugly, forgotten girl should have felt miserable, but was preserved finally from unhappiness by the wonder of it, by the long shadows and the pools of light, by the extraordinary, revealing faces of men and women, by receiving a glass of lemonade, off a silver salver, from a servant who pretended not to recognize, in their own house.

There were a great many important guests: landowners, professional men and their wives—only those who were rich, hence socially acceptable. And house guests. The bachelors' quarters were full of young men down from the country, with high spirits, good teeth, and brick-red skins.

And the dancing. And the dancing.

Mary Hare, without aspiring, loved to watch, from some familiar corner, protected by mahogany or gilt, in cave of chalcedony or malachite, peering out. From there the dancers could be seen riding the swell of music (the best that Sydney could provide) in the full arrogance of their intentions. Or, suddenly, they would lose control, whirled around by the unsuspected eddies. But willingly. As they leaned back inside the slippery funnels of the music, they would have allowed themselves to be sucked down, the laughter and the conversation trembling on their transparent teeth.

There was, in particular, the girl Helen Antill, whom some considered, in spite of her beauty and assurance—*extravagant*. Miss Antill wore a dress embroidered with little mirrors, oriental it could have been, which reflected the lights, and even, occasionally, a human feature. She carried, moreover, a fan, curiously set in a piece of irregular coral resembling a hand. The fan was of peacocks' feathers. Most unlucky.

But Miss Antill could not have been perturbed.

Mary Hare, watching, thought she might have loved something like this, just as she fell spontaneously in love with the smooth limbs of certain trees, the texture of marble, and long, immaculate legs of thoroughbred horses spanking at their exercise. Even Mrs Hare became carried away by Miss Antill's performance, and although she had at first suffered qualms on seeing the effect her guest would have upon those others present, admiration overcame her protective instincts as a mother, and she began to move quickly through her house, searching and frowning, her grey mist of chiffon trailing like an obsession after her.

"Where is Cousin Eustace?" she asked cursorily of Mary.

"It is some time since I noticed him," replied her daughter, and as she diverted her attention, realized how strange it was that she should be addressing her own mother.

Mrs Hare frowned again. At the point of sacrificing a daughter, she continued to expect that the latter should do her duty.

"You should see to it that he is not alone. When there is nobody else, you should keep him company. In fact, any young girl of serious intentions makes sure that hers is the company he wants." Then Mrs Hare sighed, realizing the difficulty of most situations. "Men do not know what they want without a little guiding."

"But I should hate to *guide* someone," replied Mary.

"The way you say it you make it sound like *drag!*" despaired the mother. "I meant to imply that a slight touch on the elbow works wonders."

"Cousin Eustace hates to be touched."

Mrs Hare preferred to interrupt a conversation that had become so physical. She would bear her cross, and in becoming thus a martyr, she was convinced that only she herself was aware of the source of her martyrdom.

So she continued the search for her relative, strengthened by her disappointments, and the vision of Miss Antill in her successful dress.

Eustace Cleugh had, in fact, performed most nobly almost all that had been expected of him that night. He had appeared to listen attentively to all those statistics with which the graziers had provided him. He had lent a sympathetic ear to graziers' wives, condemned to use up their lives on Australian soil, removed from all those material advantages which their sensibility, not to say spirituality, required. He had danced, how he had danced with the daughters. At least, his body had accepted the dictatorship of music, and his face had not let him down. But now he had gone upstairs, into the study of his Cousin Norbert Hare, to nurse his numbness, and to look through an album of engravings of German churches in the Gothic style.

Here his Cousin Eleanor found him.

"Eustace," she exclaimed, "I cannot imagine how you have allowed yourself to overlook Miss Antill. Such an exquisite dancer, and a lovely girl. I cannot rest until I see you lead her out."

And she took him by the wrist, *guiding,* as she was convinced.

Eustace Cleugh was far too well brought up to wrench himself free of gentle compulsion. All he said was, "Yes, Miss Antill is very lovely."

So Mary Hare watched their cousin brought downstairs. She watched him move out across the treacherous floor. That he was *brought,* and that he no more than *moved,* was something which perhaps only Mary noticed, but she, of course, spent so much of her time observing timid behaviour: of birds, for instance. Now here was her cousin, Eustace Cleugh, netted by the music and Miss Antill. How the mirrors in the dress flashed and reflected. Eustace did not struggle, but revolved most correctly, holding his partner; Mary alone saw how he was held. Almost the colour of nougat, his face asked the expected questions: about theatrical entertainments, the races and the weather. In the short space of his visit, he had grown surprisingly well informed on matters of local importance.

But Miss Antill seemed to remain unconvinced. As they revolved and revolved, the phrases into which she bit could have tasted peculiar. She could not quite believe in some *thing,* some failure—was it her own? Or could the bird have died before the kill? They continued, however, to revolve. As Miss Antill clutched her partner's expensive cloth and the travesty of experience, she could have been flickering, although it was attributed by almost her entire audience to the clash between light and mirrors. Such splendour as hers did not encounter uncertainties.

Then there was a pause in the music, and Mr Cleugh did behave very oddly, everybody agreed. He simply excused himself, wiped his face with a horribly white handkerchief, and walked away. It was in the end far less humiliating for Miss Antill, in spite of the slight she had suffered, for practically the whole population of the bachelors' quarters rushed upon her, to say nothing of several susceptible solicitors and elderly, unsuspected graziers.

Eustace Cleugh disappeared in the direction of the terrace. One or two ladies just noticed in the confusion of movement that dotty Mary went, or rushed, rather, after him, dropping wilted flowers as she ran, but everybody was too distracted by the scene they had just witnessed to envisage further developments of an incomprehensible nature. Besides, they had been taught firmly to suppress, like wind in company, the rise of unreason in their minds.

Eustace was on the terrace, Mary found, not quite in darkness, for the lights of the house cast a certain glow, tarnished, but comforting.

"Oh," she began, "I shall go away if you would rather."

Though she would have hated to be sent.

"No," he said. "There is no reason to go away. In this glass house. One is fully exposed, everywhere."

"Is it different, then, in other houses?"

He laughed. He sounded almost natural.

"No," he replied. "I suppose not."

"How you hated it," she said. "The dance with Miss Antill. I am sorry."

He began to tremble. If she had not pitied, she might have been shocked. But there had been moments when she had absolved even her father from being a man.

Cousin Eustace did not speak. He stood and trembled.

She touched some ivy. Painfully.

"And you will not forget it," she said.

"There comes a point where one can't remember everything," Eustace replied, with reason as well as feeling.

Then she touched the back of his hand, and he did not withdraw. Of course her skin told her immediately that she could have been a dog, but she was grateful to be accepted if only in that form. In fact, she would not have thought of expecting more, and mercifully it had never yet occurred to her to think of herself as a woman.

After a bit, he began to cough and move about without direction or elegance, like an ordinary person when nobody is there. Rather clumsily. But he did not repudiate his companion.

"Oh, dear!" He sighed, and laughed, but again roughly, and unlike him. "Do you ever crumble? Suddenly? Without warning?"

"Yes," she cried. "Oh, yes! Often. Truly."

It was most important that he should know.

But he was yawning. It could have been that he had not heard her reply, or that he had heard, and did not believe in the existence of anything outside the closed circle of himself.

She saw, however, that he was tamed, and that in future she might walk calmly, though quietly, in his vicinity, and watch him, and he would not mind. Only soon after the ball at Xanadu, Cousin Eustace resumed his tour of the world, as had always been intended, and took refuge finally on the island of Jersey, with a housekeeper, and what eventually became a famous collection of porcelain.

Even if her husband had allowed it, Mrs Hare would never have been able to forget how her cousin had insulted her guest. What she did forget, conveniently, was that she had expected of him something impossible, not to say indelicate. It was only in after life, in the regurgitation of memories, that she sometimes came across her true motive for giving the ball at Xanadu. It would drift up to the surface of her mind, almost complete, almost explicit, but always it had a horrid, quickly-to-be-rejected taste.

If Mary was less upset by Eustace Cleugh's behaviour, it was because she already expected less of the human animal, and in consequence was not surprised when he diverged from the course which other people intended he should take. The ugliness and weakness which his nature revealed at such moments were, she sensed, far closer to the truth. So she could understand and pity her cousin, even understand and pity her father, even when the latter looked at her with hate for what she saw and understood. In her time she had seen dogs receive a beating for having glimpsed their masters' souls. She was no dog, certainly, and her father had not beaten her, but there had been one occasion when he did start shooting at the chandelier.

It was a summer evening, on which the weather had not broken. The expected storm still hung heavy on the leaden mountains to the west, and the air was full of flying ants, dashing themselves against glass and flesh, and fretting off their wings in the last stages of a life over which they seemed to have no control.

As the servants, with the exception of an old coachman, who was somewhere in the region of the stables, had not yet returned from a picnic, the family had just finished helping themselves to a supper of cold fowl. This fowl had been coated, all with the best intentions, with an egg sauce, to which in the heat and the dusk the flying ants were fatally attracted, their reddish bodies squirming, with wings, without, as they died upon the baroque carcass of the anointed fowl.

"Loathsome creatures!" protested Mrs. Hare, to whom any insect was a pest.

Mary did not contribute an opinion, as the remarks of parents seldom seemed to ask for confirmation, but continued to eat, or munch, rather loudly, a crisp stick of celery, and to scratch herself, because the heat had made her prickly. In intolerable circumstances, she alone was tolerably comfortable.

To the others, it was insufferable. The light in the dining room had turned a dark brown.

Then Norbert Hare took the fowl by its surviving drumstick, and flung it through the open window, where it fell into a display of perennial phlox. It was one of his misfortunes to be led repeatedly to ruin his effects.

He was still eating. His mouth was, in fact, too full. His cheeks were swollen, and his eyes appeared almost white.

"Norbert!" cried his wife. "Whatever are the maids going to say?"

Knowing that she herself, with a lantern, would rummage amongst the phlox.

Then Norbert Hare took a loaf of bread, and flung it after the boiled fowl. He took a carving knife, and decanter of port wine, and threw.

He felt freer.

His wife began to cry.

"There," he said, for himself. "But it is never possible to free oneself. Not entirely."

His wife cried and cried.

"I am to blame," offered the daughter, in case that was what they wanted.

"If we are to decide on the objects of blame," her father shouted, "it could well be the boiled fowl."

And seemed to madden entirely.

He was running and pouncing on some intention not yet matured.

Then he seemed to remember, and went to a desk, and got out the pistols.

In the drawing-room at Xanadu, separated from the dining-room by folding doors, there was a chandelier of exceptional loveliness, which money had brought from some dismembered European house, and of which the crystal fruit now hung above antipodean soil. The great thing loomed and brooded, at times fiery, at times dreamily opalescent, but always enticing away from the endless expanse of flat thought. Mary Hare loved it, though she had always believed her passion to be secret.

Now her father went, after loading, and shot into the chandelier.

He looked very small and ridiculous standing beneath the transparent branches.

"Munching! Munch-ing!" he shouted.

And shot.

"O God, save us all!" he shouted.

And shot.

There fell at intervals an excruciating crystal rain. How much actual damage was done, it was not yet possible to estimate, although Mrs Hare did attempt spasmodically.

"There!" shouted Norbert Hare. And: "There!"

"Come! I cannot endure your father any longer!" announced the mother, and drew her daughter into a little room which was only used when the doctor came, or someone asking for money.

Then, when the door was locked, she cried, "I do not know what I have done to deserve so much!"

The daughter remained silent, for she knew she was the greater part of what her mother had to endure. Besides, it was of more interest to listen to what her father might be doing.

The sound of shots was less frequent, but boards cracked, rooms shook, the whole house seemed under the influence of his passion. He must have been running about a good deal. Until, suddenly, silence took over, its passive structure rising in tiers of indifference and layers of suffocating feathers.

"What do you think can have happened?" asked his wife, perhaps as she was expected to.

"It is probably less fun when nobody is looking," suggested the daughter, but without bearing a grudge.

"That is true," agreed the mother, startled to realize the truth had been spoken by her daughter.

For Mary was stupid, and the truth something that one generally avoided, out of respect for good taste, and to preserve peace of mind.

"I shall go out now," said Mary, at last, "and look."

"How brave you are!" the mother cried, with genuine admiration.

"I am not brave," said her daughter.

But she was unable to explain that, burning as she was, there could be no question of her dying; life itself would have been extinguished.

She found the house big and empty. The weather had changed at last, with the result that a cold wind was blowing through the rooms, scattering dead ants from the sills. The curtains tugged, swollen, at their rings.

Then her father came downstairs, very quietly, as if he had been reading in his room, and come to get a glass of water. The situation might have continued innocent enough, if it had not been for the appearance of the outraged house, and the eyes of the man who had just arrived at the bottom of the stairs.

He was looking at her, trying to engulf her in a tragedy he was preparing. Looking, and looking. It might have been horrible, if less protracted.

As it was, and perhaps realizing his error in judgment, he took the pistol she had failed to notice he was still carrying, and shot it off at his own head. And missed. A piece of plaster thumped down from a moulding on the ceiling.

The sound could have completed his exhaustion, for he tumbled immediately into a big, strait wing chair, which stood at hand. All of it he did rather clumsily and ridiculously, because it had not been thought out, or else he had lost interest in the sequence of events.

But it seemed for a moment as though she would not allow him to break the thread. She could not prevent herself from continuing to look, right into him, as he sat in the uncomfortable chair, and although he had forgiven her for the crime of being, it was doubtful whether he would ever forgive her for that of seeing.

She did not expect it, of course.

She went and picked up a pistol lying on the floor, and put it back where it had been in the first place, whether innocently, or through an inherited instinct for malice, he was too exhausted to inquire of his own mind.

He continued to sit, looking at his own waistcoat.

"All human beings are decadent," he said. "The moment we are born, we start to degenerate. Only the unborn soul is whole, pure."

As she had turned away from him, and stood picking at some flaw in the lid of the little desk, he had to torment her. He said, "Tell me, Mary, do you consider yourself one of the unborn?"

"I don't understand such things," she replied. "Not yet."

And looked round at him.

"Liar!"

He would never forgive her her eyes, and for refusing to be hurt enough.

"Oh yes, you can twist my arm if you like!" she blundered, through thickening lips, for his accusation was causing her actual physical pain. "But the truth is what I understand. Not in words. I have not the gift for words. But know."

The abstractions made her shiver. If she could have touched something—moss, for instance—or smelled the smell of burning wood.

He continued sitting in the chair, and might even have started to relent.

So, she saved him that further humiliation by going outside, and there were the stars, swimming and drowsing towards her as she put out her hands. She was walking and crying, and gulping down the effusions of light, and crying, and smearing her cheeks with the sticky backs of her rough hands.

Long after her father was dead, and disposed of under the paspalum at Sarsaparilla, and the stone split by sun and fire, with lizards running in and out of the cracks, Miss Hare acquired something of the wisdom she had denied possessing the night of the false suicide. Sometimes she would stump off into the bush in one of the terrible jumpers she wore, of brown, ravelled wool, and an old, stiff skirt, and would walk, and finally sit, always listening and expecting until receiving. Then her monstrous limbs would turn to stone, although her thoughts would sprout in tender growth of young shoots, or long loops of insinuating vines, and she would glance down at her feet, and frequently discover fur lying there from the throes of some sacri-

fice. If tears ever fell then from her saurian eyes, and ran down over
the armature of her skin, she was no longer ludicrous. She was quite
mad, quite contemptible, of course, by standards of human reason,
but what have those proved to be? Reason finally holds a gun at its
head—and does not always miss.

Often in the evening as she watched from the terrace of her deserted house for the chariot of fire, the woman wondered how her
father would have received her metamorphoses: probably with increased disgust, although a suspect visionary himself, and on one occasion at least, standing together at the same spot, she had actually
seen him twitch the veil. Now, if she had outstripped him in experience, time and silence, and the hints of nature, had given her the advantages.

So she would wait, with the breath fluctuating in her lungs, and
the blood thrilling through her distended veins. She waited on the
last evening before the person called Mrs Jolley was expected to arrive. And sure enough, the wheels began to plough the tranquil fields
of white sky. She could feel the breath of horses on her battered
cheeks. She was lifted up, the wind blowing between the open sticks
of fingers that she held extended on stumps of arms, the gold of her
father's bloodstone ring echoing the gold of trumpets. If, on the evening before the arrival of a certain person, an aura of terror had
contracted round her, she could not have said, at that precise moment, whether it was for the first time. She could not remember.
She was aware only of her present anguish. Of her mind leaving her.
The filthy waves that floated off the fragments of disintegrating
flesh.

Later, when she got up from the ground, she did not attempt to
inquire into what might have bludgeoned her numb mind and ach-
ing body, for night had come, cold and black. She bruised knuckle
on knuckle, to try to stop her shivering, and began to feel her way
through the house, by stages of brocade, and vicious gilt, by slippery tortoiseshell, and coldest, unresponsive marble.

Chapter 3

T HE FOLLOWING day, which was that of Mrs Jolley's arrival, Miss Hare did not dare look out of the house before the morning was advanced, for fear she might suffer a repetition of her experience the night before. She did not feel strong enough for that. Still, she rose as usual, in the dark, bumping and charging as she pulled her jumper on. This morning she lit the kitchen range with twigs she had gathered, and small logs sawn slowly in advance. She also swept a little in the room which she had decided the housekeeper should use. But she did not draw curtains until she saw a well-established sunlight lying on the floor. Then she waited for nothing further, but went outside, and became at once involved in many little rites, both humdrum and worshipful.

The morning glittered still with pendants of swinging light and stomachers of dew. The formidable blades of taller grasses were not yet wiped free of wet. In some cases she performed for them what later the sun would do better. But she soon gave up. It was too much for her at her age. She scattered crumbs instead, and birds came down, hobbling and bobbing at her feet, clawing at her shoulders, and in one case, holding on to the ribs of her hat. With a big pair of rusty scissors, she cut crusts of bread into the sizes she knew to be acceptable. Bending so that her skirt stuck out straight behind, she became magnificently formal, like certain big pigeons, of which one or two had descended, blue, out of the gums. All throats were moving, wobbling, and hers most of all. In agreement. In the rite of birds.

Other dedicated acts were performed in order. She drew water,

36

and set bowls. Several days earlier a snake had issued out from between the stones of the house, very black and persuasive, with tan bands along the sides. Her eyes had glistened for the splendid snake. But, although she had stood still, at once, it had failed to sense the degree of sacerdotal authority vested in the unknown woman, and returned by way of the crack in the stone, into the foundations of the house. Every morning since, she had put a saucer of milk, but the snake remained to be converted. She would wait, and eventually, of course, perfect understanding would be reached.

Morning wore away. A wind had risen, and was slashing at things, and funnelling down her front. Then she did give a slight gulp of panic, not as the result of direct physical discomfort, but because of the remoter mental pain she must suffer in the afternoon.

To say to the woman.

Miss Hare went inside.

At least she had her house. She could show her house. Its splendours would speak for her, in voices of marble and gold, to say nothing of the lesser insinuations of watered silk. So she wandered here and there, letting in always more light, and the blades of light slashed the carpets, smoking, and pillars of gold rose up in the shadows of some rooms, where they had never been before.

In a little room which had never been much used—it was, in fact, that in which she and her mother had locked themselves the night of the false suicide—she picked up a fan, of some elegance and beauty, of tortoiseshell, tufted with flamingo, which an Armenian merchant had given to her mother one winter at Aswan.

Miss Hare held the fan, but she did not dare open it on seeing her own face in the glass.

The gust of cold panic recurred.

It was time. The light told her, not her stomach, for she was seldom hungry all day long, living, it would have seemed, almost on experience; nor did clocks signal the hour at Xanadu, for clocks had stopped, and she no longer bothered to wind them up. But light told all that was ever necessary. And now the windows were gaping long and cold, with a cold, whitish light, of later afternoon.

Miss Hare began running about, doing things, and not. She did the things to her clothes that she had seen other people do. Only, she was inclined to hit, where others might have given a pat. There was nothing she could do about hair, and besides, she would be wearing the inevitable hat.

Mrs Jolley got off the bus at the post-office corner at Sarsaparilla. It could only have been Mrs Jolley, her black coat composed of innumerable panels—it appeared to be almost all seams—over what would reveal itself as the navy costume anticipated by Miss Hare. The hat was brighter, even daring, a blue blue, in spite of the mourning of which her future employer had been forewarned. From the brim was suspended, more daring, if not actually reckless, a brief mauve eye-veil. She remained, however, the very picture of a lady, waiting for identification at the bus stop, but discreetly, but brightly, and grasping her brown port.

Oh dear, then it must be done, Miss Hare admitted, and sighed.

Mrs Jolley was all the time looking and smiling, at some person in the abstract, in the rather stony street. At one corner of her mouth she had a dimple, and her teeth were modelled perfectly.

"Excuse me," began Miss Hare at last, "are you the person? Excuse me"—and cleared her throat—"are you expected at Xanadu?"

Mrs Jolley suppressed what could have been a slight upsurge of wind.

"Yes," she said, very slowly, feeling the way with her teeth. "It was some such name, I think. A lady called Miss Hare."

The latter felt tremendously presumptuous under Mrs Jolley's glance, and would have chosen to postpone her revelation.

But Mrs Jolley's white teeth—certainly no whiter had ever been seen—were growing visibly impatient. Her dimple came and went in flickers. Her expression, which might have been described as motherly by some, became suspect under the weight of its suspicion.

"I am Miss Hare," said Miss Hare.

"Oh, yes," replied the disbelieving Mrs Jolley.

And tried to fetch her teeth to the rescue.

But the brutal wind of a cold afternoon was not prepared to allow any nonsense. It flung the mauve eye-veil into Mrs Jolley's eyes, and even bashed her black coat.

"Yes," confirmed Miss Hare. "I am she."

Mrs Jolley scarcely believed what she was hearing.

"I hope you will be happy," continued the object, "at Xanadu. It is a large house. But we need only live in bits of it. Move around as we choose, for variety's sake."

Mrs Jolley began to accompany her mentor, over the stones, in shoes which she had purchased for the journey. Black. With a sensible strap. But, even so, she thought her ankles might not stand the walk, and the fangs of the road metal were eating through her soles.

"You haven't a car, then?" she asked.

"No," said Miss Hare. "No cars."

Level with the Godbolds' shed, the blackberry canes snatched at Mrs Jolley's coat.

"We never owned a car," Miss Hare was saying. "Even in the days of my father. Naturally cars were only beginning. But horses. My father fancied horses; he was quite splendid when he drove his greys four-in-hand."

Mrs Jolley could not believe any of this. Remembering the trams, she could have cried.

"In our family," she said, "everybody has their own car."

"Oh," said Miss Hare. "No. No cars."

The sound of the two women's breathing would intermingle distressingly at times. Each wished she could have repudiated the connection.

"It is a satisfaction to a mother," said Mrs Jolley, on twisting ankles, "to know that each one of them—three girls—is each settled comfortable."

"Of course," agreed Miss Hare.

She could not believe, though. Not a bit.

Then they walked down the track which the Council had begun to call an avenue, and which led to Xanadu. Arriving at the end, the employer guided her companion through the fence, and they began the less tortuous, the longer of the short cuts.

As her responsibilities loomed, Miss Hare drew ahead. Mrs Jolley followed, occasionally hearing something tear. The silence was shocking in the undergrowth.

In the circumstances, the nascent green of oaks and elms, massed to overwhelm the scrub, issued too shrill, the grace-notes of crab and plum blossom, sprinkled at intervals on black nets of twigs, too sickeningly poignant.

Mrs Jolley remarked, "A good thing I put me lisle stockings on."
Her mauve eye-veil was less gay.

"The burrs do prick a little, but they pick off quite easily," Miss
Hare thought to offer over her shoulder.

She had grown nervous, as if, at the back of her mind, there was
something dreadful she could not remember.

They went on.

"We shall arrive soon now," she encouraged.

They went on.

"There!" her voice revealed.

Mrs Jolley did not answer, almost failed to look up.

They climbed the approach. Under the stranger's feet the tessel-
lated floor of the veranda sounded hollow as never before.

But the house was hollowest.

Miss Hare had opened the front door. They had gone in. They
had stood for ages.

"Well," Mrs Jolley said at last, "it is easy to see it's a long time
since you had a lady here."

Nor did the voices of Xanadu protest. They agreed in all coldness
of stone.

"A house is not the less for what you make it," said Miss Hare.

"Nor any more," added the darker voice of Mrs Jolley.

Neither could have offered adequate explanation of what she had
just said. Each saw what she saw, or rather, Miss Hare was beginning to remember what she had forgotten. The veins in her temples
were writhing. It was as if some stranger with sly eyelids had touched
the real door, with a finger, and there stood the interior.

"That was the drawing-room," she said, the tense forced upon
her. "And the dining-room through the folding doors."

But forced most brutally.

They were standing in the present, in the late hours of an afternoon in spring, when the light can be merciless. The white light fell
amongst the furniture, where a bandaged memory awaited diagnosis.

"I have never seen anything like it," confessed Mrs Jolley, withdrawing as far as possible into her clothes.

Where time had not slashed, the light was finishing the job. Cabi-
nets and little frivolous tables seemed to splinter at a blow. Even
solid pieces in marquetry, and the buhl octopus, were stunned.

Catching on to the thread of their original intention, the two women strayed here and there, but always retreating. Now a shutter had begun to bang. Old birds' nests, lying on the Aubusson, or what had become, rather, a carpet of twigs, dust, mildew and the chrysalides of insects, trapped guilty feet with soft reminders. On one side of the dining room, where weather had torn the slates from an embrasure in the course of some historic storm, an elm had entered in. The black branches of the elm sawed. The early leaves pierced the more passive colours of human refinement like a knife. The little rags of blue sky flickered and flapped drunkenly. In places rain had gushed, in others trickled, down the walls, and over marble, now the colour of rotten teeth.

"Or places where dogs have pissed," Miss Hare noticed, and sighed.

"I beg yours?" asked Mrs Jolley, wondering.

But her employer did not answer—her thoughts were her own, whether she cared to utter them or not—so the housekeeper saved up what she believed she had heard, to let it ripen on the shelves of her mind before she took it down for use.

At last Miss Hare cleared her throat, and that, too, sounded dusty —she was really quite exhausted. She said, "I think I shall take you to your room now."

As the stair wound upward, by slow convolutions, through the well of light, its loveliness tortured the throat of the owner.

"I would sit here sometimes," she said, "and listen to the music, and watch the dancers. Oh, it was splendid down there."

As the stair wound upward, past the closed doors, passages tunnelled off, into distance and a squeaking of mice.

"Of course, a great many of these rooms," she said, and waved, practical again, "have not been opened for years. There was no reason why they should have been. Not after the death of my mother. She died at the beginning of the war. The second, yes, it was the Second War. It was Father who went during the first. And Mother, I found her sitting in her chair. But this is not the time to tell family history. And on the stairs."

"I am a mother," said Mrs Jolley, "and am always glad to hear of anybody in like circumstances."

Her ring chinked on the wrought iron. Despite shortness of breath, she did, and would act firmly. Her corset could not assure enough as she followed up the stairs. She would act as befitted a mother and a lady; it was only to be hoped the two duties would not clash.

"Here," said Miss Hare, "is the room I have prepared. I have made the bed. Although people have different ideas on the making of a bed. There," she said.

Would the door open?

Mrs Jolley wished it would not, and that they might be left, instead, looking at each other on the landing, however unsatisfactory that solution might be.

But the door did open, easily, even, one would have said, eagerly.

"Well," said Mrs Jolley, "we shall see."

And smiled.

She had a blue eye that would see just so far and no farther, which was perhaps why she could recover while still professing shock. Miss Hare hoped that her housekeeper's face was kind, but suspected that the dimple had not bewitched more than the one man.

Mrs Jolley did not know where to begin, and would stand kneading her bare arms, as if they might not have got their final shape. In that spring weather her milky arms were dapple-blue against the silk jumper—she had knitted it herself—oyster-toned, but sagging now.

Mrs Jolley was a lady, as she never tired of pointing out. She would repeat the articles of her faith for anybody her instinct caught doubting. She would not touch an onion, she insisted; not for love. But was partial to a fluffy sponge, or butter sandwich, with non-pareils. A lady could never go wrong with pastel shades. Or Iceland poppies. Or chenille. She liked a good yarn, though, with another lady, at the bus stop, or over the fence. She liked a drive in a family car, to nowhere in particular, but looking out, in a nice hat, at faces on a lower level. Then the mechanism with which her superior station had fitted her would cause her head to move ever so slightly, to convey her disbelief.

She preferred to believe, however, and so Mrs Jolley would go to the pictures. To sit at the pictures sucking a lolly—not a hard one—after dropping the paper, along with memories and intentions, under the seat, was to indulge in sheerest velvet. It was a pity, though, about the hard lollies; the smell of a hot, moist caramel almost drove her nuts. But she would sit, and the strangest situations would pass muster as life. That lean young fellow, in crow's-feet and leather pants, might just have reached down, and put his hand—it made her lolly stick; and Ava and Lana, despite proportions and circumstances, could have been a couple of her own girls. Best of all was a picture about a mother. She knew by heart the injustices to expect, not to mention the retribution, so that, at the end, the Wurlitzer rising from its well only completed her apotheosis. When she smelled the *vox humana*'s rose and violet breath, and felt the little hammers striking on her womb, then she was, indeed, fulfilled, and could forget her hubby, who had died in the lounge at ten p.m., as she was handing him his second cup of tea. Grave as that injustice was, she had survived, and, it appeared, might have experienced enough of life and dreams to parry any further blows.

Miss Hare was afraid she might be afraid of her housekeeper. She said, "I hope you will get used to things."

"I miss the trams," Mrs Jolley replied.

The clang of them was in her voice, and in her eye, the melancholy plume of violet sparks.

"Oh dear," said Miss Hare, "I cannot say I was ever attached to a tram."

"I miss Saturday evening," Mrs Jolley said. "Dropping in at Merle's, or Dot's, or Elma's. Elma is the youngest—married a stoker, not that he is not a gentleman, because none of my girls would never ever have entertained the idea of anything else but a gentleman."

"I am surprised you could bear to leave them," said Miss Hare, almost not loud enough.

"Ah," said Mrs Jolley, and took the mop, "that is life, if you know what I mean."

Then she screwed the mop in the bucket, and took it out, and looked at the head.

"Or death," she said.

Miss Hare was terrified.

"As if it was my fault," said Mrs Jolley. "Sitting in his own chair."

"A chair makes it seem more natural," Miss Hare ventured to suggest.

Remembering her mother, who had died in similar circumstances, thus she comforted herself.

"I can just imagine you and your mum," Mrs Jolley said, and laughed. "Living here amongst the furniture. Like a couple of mice."

"Oh, there was Peg, too, and William Hadkin."

"Peg who?"

"I can't remember her name. If we ever knew it. She always seemed old. And had always been here. When the maids left—after the troubles overtook us—Peg stayed, and became a friend. And died, too. But after Mother. I was quite alone then."

"And who was the gentleman you was speaking of?"

"William was a coachman. He was very deaf."

Miss Hare paused.

"He was what they call *rather simple*. Which means that what one knows is of a different kind. Actually, William knew an awful lot. And was not so deaf. I did not like him."

"And this Mr Hadkin, did he die too?"

"No. He simply went away."

"Strike a light!" said Mrs Jolley. "No wonder! What did all you people live on?"

"Things," said Miss Hare, and yawned. "Bread, for instance. Bread is lovely. I love to tear the ends off, and eat it just like that. Going along. And give it to the birds. It is so convenient. But, of course, we had the little allowance from my cousin, Eustace Cleugh, of which I wrote you. Certainly it was not very much, and that was discontinued in the war. Oh, I forgot. There was the goat. I had a goat, and would milk her. Yes, I missed her."

"What happened to the goat?"

"Please don't ask me!" cried Miss Hare. "I don't know!"

"All *right!*" said Mrs Jolley, whose turn it was to be afraid.

In that house.

But Miss Hare was sad rather than afraid. She could not answer questions. Questions were screws that spiralled down into the brain. She looked at the bucket of grey water, from which the woman's mop was spreading ineffectual puddles. The woman whose three daughters' husbands had built with bricks, boxes in which to live. So childish. For the brick boxes of the daughters' husbands would tumble like the games of children. Only memories were indestructible.

So Miss Hare snorted—she was bored, besides, with Mrs Jolley—and went off into the passages of Xanadu.

But memories also tormented. They flapped like old rags of curtains, the priceless ones with gold thread, and moths flew out, always grey, or night-coloured, scattering their suffocating down.

"We must wrap up our furs, Mary," Mrs Hare had said, "very carefully, now that summer is here, in sheets of the *Herald*. And put them in strong canvas bags, with draw-necks. I shall feel uneasy otherwise."

Mrs Hare had remained mostly happy, right to the end, in the ritual of a past life.

And Peg would run, on her sticks of legs, and say from between her naked gums, which her mistress permitted, because, well, of everything, "Yes, m'mm. No one likes to have moths on their mind. But leave it to me. No, miss, I will see to it."

And the servant would show the canvas bags, their necks well and truly drawn. Yes, those geese were dead, the daughter saw, and stuffed with the balls of paper Peg had put, to simulate. But the mother was pacified.

Mrs Hare, gentle in her youth, distinguished in maturity, had become a horse of polished ivory in her old age. She would sit quite still for half an hour, then suddenly toss her head, at a thought, or fly. It was her long, refined face that gave the impression, and long, ivory teeth, which she loved to exercise on the fingers of cinnamon toast brought to her by Peg. Afterwards she would continue to sit, while her elderly, refined stomach rumbled with tea and toast, and the waning light worked still further, with uncanny Chinese skill, at the polished portrait of an ivory horse.

Sometimes she would walk through what remained of the gardens, leaning on her stumpy daughter's arm, but she did not notice very much. She preferred to remember social triumphs and the Borromean Isles.

Once she asked the daughter, "Where is the grotto, Mary? The grotto that your father had them build out of shells. Or was it lumps of rock crystal?"

The daughter grunted, for, after all, nothing more was expected of her.

Once Mrs Hare started to complain.

"I used to hope my daughter would become an ambassador's wife. She would have long, beautiful legs, and carry a fan, and manage other people's conversation. In the end there is nothing one has managed. Not even of one's own.

"Still," she continued more cheerfully, "you would not have

been walking with me in the garden, in those circumstances, and I might have fallen over on my own, and broken something."

Again the daughter grunted, because what else could she have done?

Then the mother began to hit the grass.

"Horrid, horrid tufts!" she cried, beating the tussocks of paspalum with her stick, so that the tassels of the grass trembled.

"Don't!" begged the daughter. "Please!"

Such impotent caprice was, at least, quickly diverted.

"But do not think I am not devoted to you, Mary," insisted the mother. "I can truly, honestly say I do love everybody now. Even your father."

For Mrs Hare, whose passions had always been watery, it was perhaps easier.

"Even one's disappointments seem, at the end, to have a kind of meaning," she said towards sunset.

And would have squeezed her daughter's arm if she had had the strength.

Instead, they went inside, the disappointing daughter, and the mother who was, in the end, supported by her disappointments.

Months later, looking at the figure of the dead woman seated so naturally in her chair, the daughter cried because she could not mourn in an approved manner. With passion, perhaps, but that the mother would hardly have appreciated or understood. So she mourned life, instead, such as she herself suspected it of being, from sudden rages of the sky, and brown gentleness of young ferns.

It was fortunate that Peg had been there, because it was Peg who knew what to do. She sent William to Sarsaparilla, and the postmistress telephoned, and some men arrived to take the body. It was a day of rain, and the hall had smelt of wet raincoat quite a while afterwards.

Those were the last dealings Mary Hare had with her mother.

For Peg had said, "Don't you bother to go to the funeral, Miss Mary, if you feel it will upset you. Who will hold you if you take a turn? We'll sit here together, you and me, and eat a piece of bread and dripping in front of the stove. And let the parson look after things; that's what he is there for."

Peg, although an elderly woman, had preserved some link with childhood, which allowed her to recognize the forms of reality through the rough sheath of appearance. She remained an admirable companion. Mary loved Peg. She would sit and rub her own wrinkles, and watch her maid's tranquil face: that of an elder sister in steel-rimmed spectacles, a sister who knew approximately the plan of an outside world, but who had not forgotten all the games.

Because she was of that district, Peg used to go about a lot. She would ride her bicycle at the hills, and it was surprising how she got to the top. Such a frail thing. Not much more than the sawing sound of her own washed-out, starched dress. Peg laundered and cleaned to perfection, but cooked badly. She liked to make jam, and render down beeswax, and usually smelled of one or the other. She would suddenly appear from under beds, holding a pad of waxy cloth, when a person least expected. In her steel-rimmed spectacles. In a dress that had once been pale blue, now almost white.

"Read to me, Peg," her mistress Mary Hare would command.

"Read yourself!" Peg advised, and laughed. "What shall I read, ever?"

"I can see it better if you read it out. Do, Peg!" begged Mary Hare. "Let us read Anthony Hordern's catalogue."

"Dear, you are a caution!" Peg had to laugh.

She was rather pale around the eyes.

Peg liked best to read the Bible, but not aloud, as her mistress did not care for it. The maid was always busy with the Gospels. She found the Epistles too dry, and did not go much on the Revelations— in fact, she showed no inclination to discuss that end of her battered book.

"You ought to be having a study of this," Peg used to say, glancing up from her Bible.

She had always worn an exposed look on account of her pale eyelids, but her innocence had protected her.

"Oh dear, no!" protested her mistress, almost in fear. "I know that that is nothing for me."

"It is for everybody," Peg would insist earnestly.

"Not quite. It is not for me."

"But you won't try it. How have you ever found out?"

"I will find out what I am to find out, in my own way, and in my own time. I am different," maintained Mary Hare.

"Yes," sighed Peg. "Different and the same."

She could not marvel at it enough.

Although the two women were in many ways not unlike, Peg was without that arrogance which snared her mistress frequently. Mary Hare loved Peg, but she loved her own arrogance. It was her great pride, and if nobody else recognized her jewel, then, she would still deck herself. That way she achieved distinction, perhaps even beauty, she was vain enough to hope.

But Peg was not taken in. She would say in her slightly gritty voice, "You are not flying into one of your tantrums, Miss Mary?"

And Peg was always right, the way glass is, and water—all that is blameless.

Which made it the more desperate when Mary Hare went into Peg's room, and saw that her friend had died. Just after dressing. On a dry morning. Peg had lain down again on the bed, in her dress that had once been a brighter colour. There she lay, very brittle, like a branch of one of the good-smelling herbs, rosemary, or thyme, or the lemon-scented verbena, that people used to break off to put away.

After a while the mistress dared to touch her maid. Then, she knew, at last, she was, indeed, alone. She stayed a long time in a corner of the room, looking, and it was only in the course of the morning that she remembered William Hadkin.

William was somebody Mary Hare had never taken to, perhaps because, on the night of her father's shooting match, when all the other servants were still away at the picnic, he had remained in the grooms' quarters, together with his deafness. That deafness of William's was something Mary had never been able to believe in, because of the thundering of her own emotions on the night in question. Yet, he had remained faithful, and in the days of her mother would take them for little drives in an old buggy that had survived. And on a pittance. Though, of course, he was old, nor ate, nor needed very much. By the time Mrs Hare died, he had practically given up shaving, because of a tender skin, yet was always seen in the same length of stubble, with the same rivulet of spittle in the same white ravine. He had the same smell, too, of most old men. Which again could have been a reason why Miss Hare had not taken to him. Old men, on the whole, are smellier than old women.

It was William, of course, that his mistress told of Peg's death.

"Well, yes," he said. "I was reckoning she would die. There was nothing to her."

He was greasing a strap of harness, for which there was no longer any use, but it helped to keep him in practice.

"I would not have let myself think," began Mary Hare.

"That was what all you people was such artists at," said William Hadkin, stroking his leather.

"What do you mean?" asked Miss Hare.

She began to tremble, but not with rage.

"As far as I can see, lookin' back and all," William said, "you was the race of pretenders."

"Some of us had imagination, if that is what you mean."

"To set the house on fire without the matches!"

"That is enough, William," said Mary Hare, as she had heard parents. "You must go about Peg."

"All right! All right!" he said. "Don't agitate me!"

He stood looking at the holes in the strap.

"I wonder you stayed if you could not bear us," his mistress said.

"I stayed," he said, "because I got used to it. There's a lot of that sort of thing going on, you know."

Because his mistress was always the first to recognize the truth, there was really nothing for her to say.

The last and worst encounter with William Hadkin occurred a few weeks after her maid's death. She came across him just after he had killed a cock. There was the bird's head, shamefully detached and dead, while William watched and laughed as the body danced out the last steps of life in a shambles of its own blood.

Mary Hare stood very still. She could not find the strength to move even when her boots were sprinkled with the cock's blood.

William observed.

"Well," he said, laughing, "you've gotta eat, if it's only an old stringy rooster."

And continued to laugh.

"See," he said, "what I meant the other day? The rooster got so used to it he can dance without his bally head."

"The way I see it, you are a murderer," accused Mary Hare.

"What! To kill a cock for you to eat?"

"There are ways and ways of killing."

"That is something you should know."

"How? I?"

"Ask your dad."

Mary Hare turned so pale. She remained standing by the woodshed long after the groom had gone about other business. She was left looking at the wattles of the dead cock.

Soon after that William Hadkin, without a word, sorted his thoughts apparently, and disappeared from Xanadu. Now, at last, I shall be free, and all to the good, murmured Mary Hare, afraid. But remembered the goat, and at once her spirits were restored.

The goat had appeared already before Peg's death. From where it had come was never discovered. A white doe heavy in kid, it would follow the women for company, choosing its leaves and grass with a certain finical air. After the doe had been delivered of a dead buck, Peg said they should milk their goat, which Mary Hare proceeded to do. She lived for it. In time her mind grew equal to the tranquil wisdom of the goat-mind, and as she squatted in the evening to milk her doe, after they alone were left, their united shadow would seem positively substantial. So much so, the woman's love began to conflict with her reasoning, and she grew quite frantic that something might happen to the animal: some disaster to follow those which she herself had been permitted to outlive, or, simply, that it might decide to leave.

So, when night began to fall, the mistress would run to shut her creature in a little tipsy shed, within sight of the kitchen, on the edge of the yard. Heaping boughs and pouring endearments, she would padlock her goat every night, and return, and return, to see whether her love might not have vanished in the course of some devilish conjuring act. But there the goat would be. As she shielded her lamp, the white mask glimmered at her through the dark. The amber eyes pacified her fears, and the long lip would move in what she knew was sympathy.

Even on the morning of the mistress's severest trial, the abstraction of a goat's mask continued to communicate. Even though the goat itself had become a skull and shred of hide in the ruins of the black and smoking shed.

How she herself survived the holocaust of her discovery, Mary Hare could never be sure. But the morning was kind. Leaves were laid upon her face. The earth was soft to her trembling knees. For she went off into the scrub almost immediately, and remained there how long nobody was able to tell her, because nobody knew that she had gone. She remained there probably two or three days, for she returned stiff and scratched, hungry, at least for one who was almost never visited by hunger, and anxious to recall even the painful reason for her absence.

As she sat chewing a crust of stale bread, for which she had immediately rummaged in the crock, she had to suppose:

Eventually I shall discover what is at the centre, if enough of me is peeled away.

Never in her life, she felt, had she reasoned so lucidly, with the result that she swallowed a whole lump of softened bread.

Mrs Jolley was in two minds.

It could have been the cobwebs. She would drag them down. They could have been ropes. They could have been chains. Then she would pick, and flick, not to say dash, and bash, all thumbs and fingers, elbows too, as she struggled to divest herself. But would never be free. The grey skeins clung, like a sense of guilt.

"Who isn't nuts!" she would cry at times. "But, of course, a person can always give notice—tomorrow, or the day after, any day of the week."

Nobody would have thought to accuse Mrs Jolley of not being rational at every pore, even at moments when, netted in cobweb, clamped with bobby-pins, teeth upstairs in the tumbler, her answer might stumble. As she pursed her lips, and turned her head, to disengage the reluctant words, was she guarding a secret, or merely having trouble with her lolly?

At least she would remain a lady, whatever else might come in doubt.

For the mirrors had begun to follow her down the passages, and on one occasion, she had been compelled to finish a flight of stairs at the run. For no obvious reason. Her legs had simply taken over, and her calves, still strong, and firm, and glossy, had bulged rather frantically; her breasts were jumping under the corset by the time she reached the top.

"Everybody has their off days," Mrs Jolley liked to say.

When, for instance, one of her eyes—blue for mothers—would water from the corner.

"I am so afraid you are not happy at Xanadu," remarked Miss Hare—it was at breakfast, over the crispies, in the kitchen.

"It is not that I am not happy," answered Mrs Jolley. "I am always happy, of course, more or less. It is that a lady does expect something different."

Miss Hare mashed her crispies.

"What?"

"Oh, you know," said Mrs Jolley, "a home, and a Hoover, and kiddies' voices."

"I do not know," replied Miss Hare. "This is my life. This is my home."

And she munched the crispies.

"You are that hard at times," Mrs Jolley protested, "and unwilling to understand."

Miss Hare munched her crispies.

"When a loved one passes on, it is as if you was lost for a bit. See?"

Miss Hare would not. She was familiar with the core of rock she must acquire to match Mrs Jolley.

"As if a bit of you went with him. And if you don't follow, too, it is because of a sense of duty to others. I once read in a horoscope" —here Mrs Jolley picked the cloth—"that my sense of duty is very, very highly developed."

"I am not preventing you from following whoever you wish to follow," Miss Hare replied. "If that is what you mean."

"You know that I was referring to my late hubby," said Mrs Jolley, "and you will not hurt my feelings, however hard you try."

That face!

"Oh, dear, it is breakfast," sighed Miss Hare.

Mrs Jolley went off into laughter. She laughed, and laughed, and laughed.

"I will not ask what you find so amusing," announced Miss Hare.

"People are that funny!" Mrs Jolley laughed.

Her throat had knots in it, almost a goitre, and farther down was the cleft upon which the eyes of her late husband, presumably, had rested, whether in approval or disgust.

Miss Hare, who had finished her crispies, turned the plate upside down as usual.

Mrs Jolley had stopped laughing. Very, very patiently she said, "You are a dirty girl. That is what *you* are!"

And stood back to look.

"A habit is a habit," said Miss Hare.

"Dirty is dirty," replied her companion.

"Mrs Jolley, two people cannot live together unless they respect each other's habits. That is something I have learnt by painful degrees in my relationships with birds and animals."

"I am not a bird, or a animal," Mrs Jolley replied. "I am a—"

"No. I know what you are. Please, do not tell me!" Miss Hare begged.

"You do not know me," Mrs Jolley said, "any more than you don't know nothing at all."

"No," Miss Hare agreed. "You are often right."

"I know what I am," said Mrs. Jolley, "and more's the pity. My late husband thought he knew, but didn't. He thought he knew. Oh, yes, he knew everything. He had taken night courses, and collected stamps. He was paying off a cyclopaedia, for years, in the oak cabinet, beside the settee."

Quite suddenly Mrs Jolley began to cry.

Miss Hare sat as still as she could, and watched.

"All I did," Mrs Jolley cried, "was to make him a clean and comfortable home, and yet, that night when I handed him his cup of tea, you would of said I had committed a crime."

Miss Hare watched. The kitchen at Xanadu was one of those big, old, black kitchens which swallow up, but Miss Hare was never swallowed. She was feeling very bright now.

"Do you mean that your husband blamed you for his death?"

Mrs Jolley almost choked.

"You are that hard!" she protested. "And this house! You can hear your own thoughts ticking, along with the mouldy furniture. I will leave, of course. But, in the circumstances, not yet."

Then she stopped. She seemed to have immediate control over her emotions, or almost anything, if she wished. Mrs Jolley was what Miss Hare supposed they called a practical woman.

"There!" said Mrs Jolley. "Finished now!"

And pursed her mouth up.

But Miss Hare was not finished. Her train of thought, she feared, had only started. If she had not been so fascinated, she would have retreated from the presence of Mrs Jolley, who was responsible.

"What you have just told, has made me remember something," she said. "Only one person ever blamed me for his death."

"Who?"

Mrs Jolley took possession of Miss Hare's disgusting, fascinating, down-turned plate.

"My own father."

"You have not spoken much about your dad," Mrs Jolley slowly realized.

"There is so much to tell, and almost all of it painful," said Miss Hare.

"But your own father."

"A long time ago. He died most horribly. By drowning in a cistern."

"Where?"

"Out there. Across the yard. It collects the rain-water from the roof, and in those days was allowed to remain open. It was only closed later, on account of the mosquitoes."

"And your father fell in?"

"Oh, there are some people—I might as well say from the beginning—will tell you other things. My father was said to be unstable."

"And you saw it?"

"I sometimes wonder exactly what."

Norbert Hare had experienced his moments of illumination. Doors had opened once or twice in music, or he had turned a corner on an Italian street, or descended dizzily, breathlessly, his vision grown milky and unreliable, from a too reckless encounter in the stone branches of some Gothic forest. On occasions release had even come simply by watching the line of hills beyond his property of Xanadu, although he was inclined to suspect deliverance by inexpensive means. Whatever the source of his experience, he was, however, aware of a splendour that he himself would never achieve except by instants, and rightly or wrongly, came to interpret this as failure. He would sometimes laugh, unpleasantly, and what seemed irrelevantly, to those who heard, with the result that many of his acquaintances and neighbours became convinced that Norbert was mad. Only his daughter, Mary, obviously more than a little dotty herself, sensed his dilemmas. She might even have understood them if she had been allowed.

But the mere idea was preposterous.

One steamy morning in summer, at the time of year when the whole world was living palpably under grass, in a crushing scent of crushed grass, in a mercilessly gentle murmuring of doves, Mary Hare rose up, actually, visibly, out of her father's thoughts. At one of those moments when two people would give their souls to escape each other, neither could begin. There she was, rooted in his path, where it led beneath the camphor laurels, and meandered on into the yard.

"You, Mary!" exclaimed Norbert Hare, the sharp corners of his mouth outlined in dry, white salt.

There was no need for him to give further expression to his feelings.

Of course, she could not answer. She stood and twisted a stalk of grass.

A trick of light had endowed her with what could have been a shadow of beauty under the old goffered bonnet she was wearing: a country beauty, botched and brown, and quickly gone. But her father would not allow. He might have been denying the possibility for years, for now he said, from a long way off, but very distinctly, as some sounds will convey themselves in a stillness and from a distance, "Ugly as a foetus. Ripped out too soon."

Then their emotions were whirling, the spokes of whitest light smashing, the hooks grappling together, hatefully.

The sweat was running down her body, she could feel, in molten streams. She caught sight of his tightening mouth, and his throat strung with gristle.

"If you think we cannot put an end to it! But I am the one to choose!"

Whether she had heard this as she was walking away, she had never been quite certain; perhaps she would have liked to hear it.

But a stench was rising from the flesh of bruised grass. She was being surely suffocated under a pall of leaves.

Till his great voice began to call through a megaphone of stone.

She went back then, and realizing that it came from the cistern, looked in to see him treading water. The hair hung above his eyes in a straight, black, wet fringe. His eyes were awful—very pale, and far-seeing—as his voice, under the influence of cold and fear, continued to reproduce a desperate glug-glug of water. How cold the water was she could remember from once dipping her hand, in time of drought, into a bucketful a gardener had drawn up.

And now her father.

"Get some-thing, Mar-y!" Her dream seemed to be giving tongue. "Some-one!"

At the same time it sounded silly. He was like some spaniel thrown in against its will, and whose genuine dog-tragedy appeared to be drowning in comical acts.

She ran, though. She got a pole; it was an old, bleached clothes-prop. She stood above him, away up, in the light, on the rim of the cistern.

Then he appeared more afraid than before, as if she were looking truly monstrous from that height and angle, as she held the pole towards him.

He was crying now, like a little boy, out of pale, wet mouth.

"Some-one!" he was crying. "Mary! Don't! Have some pity! For God's sake! Run!"

Although rigid, her pole was merciful, but he warded it off with his hands, which were blue, she observed, and he would bob under, and return, each time his deathly fringe falling into place again on his forehead.

So she gathered up her dress at last, holding it bundled over her stomach, and ran, by whatever made her. She was two beings.

She ran through the deserted morning. It laid clammy hands upon her. She fell once, bumping along gravel. The house could have been a shell from which even the echo of distance had withdrawn. The little frail parasols, which protected the complexions of the roses, were on that morning untended by the second gardener.

By the time Mary Hare fetched William Hadkin and a boy, it was plain her father's folly had caught up with him; regret was of no assistance. He was gone by then. A frog plopped. A leaf fluttered, floated. When they finally dredged him up from under the black water, his pale eyes looked fearfully at those who had failed to rescue him, and for the first time the daughter realized how very similar his expression was to one of her own.

After that, Sarsaparilla learned how Norbert Hare had fallen into the tank at Xanadu. Although those who pulled him out said they would have taken a bet he had jumped, and others had even begun to consider whether—but that would have been uncharitable, not to say unthinkable. So there the matter rested, or was hushed up, rather, for the sake of a proper funeral.

At first the widow was not expected to recover from her grief. Or was it shock?

"How I feel for your poor mother!" said Mrs Jolley. "Even now. Even after she has passed on. Only one who has been a wife and mother can ever fully sympathize."

"There are those who believe that they, and only they, can understand a dog."

"I beg yours?" asked Mrs Jolley.

"Nothing," replied Miss Hare, and laughed into her cup. "We were talking about my mother. She felt for herself, I think. More than enough."

"You are a hard one!"

"I was hardened.

"But not all hard," added the blotchy woman, after a second's thought, and softer. "Or I would be dead of it."

"Well, I never!"

"Oh, there is a great deal that I truly, truly love."

"Are you a Christian?"

"Ah," sighed Miss Hare. "It would not be for me to say, even if I understood exactly what that means."

"I am," said Mrs Jolley. "I attended the C. of E. ever since I was a kiddy."

And would batter somebody to prove it.

"I mean," persisted the housekeeper, "didn't anybody bother with your religious education?"

Miss Hare was too embarrassed to answer.

"So as you can believe. You do believe in *something*, don't you?"

Miss Hare hesitated. Then she said, very slowly, "I believe. I cannot tell you what I believe in, any more than what I am. It is too much. I have no proper gift. Of words, I mean. Oh, yes, I believe! I believe in what I see, and what I cannot see. I believe in a thunderstorm, and wet grass, and patches of light, and stillness. There is such a variety of good. On earth. And everywhere."

"But what is over it?" Mrs Jolley had to burst out.

"That!" Miss Hare cried. "That! I would rather you did not ask me about such things."

She had got up, and was swaying and trembling, so that Mrs Jolley became afraid. How she hated that blotchy face. Just supposing it had a fit!

"I am sorry I started all this if it is too much for you," the housekeeper said, very firmly, not looking any more, and controlling her voice.

"Oh, no," breathed Miss Hare.

And went away.

Mrs Jolley listened, hoping she might hear a body fall. She hoped Miss Hare might die, even. Then all that was bright and solid, all that was known and vouched-for must prevail.

So Mrs Jolley rushed at the oven, to bake a cake, although it was not a day of celebration, but she liked to bake, a pink cake for choice, with nonpareils and something written on it. With the Mothers' Union and the Ladies' Guild, with the Fellowships Senior and Junior, pink was always popular, and what is popular is safe.

Mrs Jolley sang and baked. She loved to sing the pinker hymns. She would even sing those of which she did not know the words. She sang and baked. And saw pink. She loved the Jesus Christ of long pink face and languid curls, in words and windows. All was right then. All the homes and kiddies saved. All was sanctified by cake.

At Xanadu the great kitchen almost cracked black open.

Mrs Jolley sang and baked. Brick by brick her edifice rose, but a nice sandwich, of course. Round. Whereas it was the square brick homes which she celebrated. And populated. With her mind she placed the ladies and the kiddies—not so many gentlemen—as if they had been sandwich flags: the little girls, with their fresh frocks and tiny rings and vanity bags; the lovely little boys, with freckles and quiffs, and teeth that too much cake had destroyed. Mrs Jolley sang and praised. To destroy or to save was the same when you had paid the premium.

As the time approached to ice her cake, the smell of delicious baking and support of family morality had made this woman strong. So she must remain; it was only nerves that had caused her to falter a moment, and the company of that poor dill.

Ah, dear, you had to laugh, though!

When Miss Hare returned, Mrs Jolley had burst open. Her white teeth were gashing the kitchen.

"Will you share the joke?" asked the mistress.

"Would I share!" Mrs Jolley rocked.

Until Miss Hare had to smile in self-defence.

"Ah, dear, I am bad!" Mrs Jolley cried, and laughed. "That is what I am!"

She looked at Miss Hare. If she had not been breathless, she would have blown down the whole dusty house of cards on the owner's head, and walked away into the perspective of certainty.

Chapter 4

A T W H A T stage she had begun to fear Mrs Jolley, Miss Hare was not sure, though she thought it probably dated from the morning when the housekeeper had presented her with a pink cake, and on it written, really most beautifully, in fancy script:

FOR A BAD GIRL

"What a beautiful cake!" Miss Hare had exclaimed, with something like horror.

"I would not claim to be artistic if my son-in-law, the stoker— he is the husband of Elma, the youngest—had not told me that I was," Mrs Jolley replied.

But she coughed for decency's sake.

"You must not mind the joke," she added. "Two ladies living together should cultivate a sense of humour."

As she watched her employer, the milky dimple was in its place.

"Oh, how I agree!"

Miss Hare laughed, and her right leg stiffened as she kicked the kitchen flags with her heel.

Then Mrs Jolley lowered her eyelids.

Yes, it was from the moment Mrs Jolley lowered her eyelids that Miss Hare had begun to feel afraid. Of course, she did not fear for her person. She could come to no physical harm; she was too old, too ugly, too poor, too unimportant in anybody's life. But she did sense some danger to the incorporeal, the more significant part of her. Time and isolation had rendered this, she had felt until now, practically indestructible. Even history, wars had not coerced her inner being. Except for her relationship with her father, the brief unpleasantness with William Hadkin, and the death of her poor goat, she had had little experience of evil. Newspapers she never read; living, not reading about it, had been her life. So the world had revolved on the axis with which she had provided it, until Mrs Jolley brought the virtues to Xanadu.

Days after the lettering had been consumed, Miss Hare was haunted by the pink cake. She must, she *would* understand it, though there were pockets of thought which her mind refused to enter, like those evil thickets in which might be found little, agonizing tufts of fur, broken swallows' eggs, or a goat's rational skull.

How much Mrs Jolley knew, it was difficult to tell. She would lower her eyelids and go disguised. There was always the veil of conversation—Miss Hare dreaded it most of all: the piles of brick that Mrs Jolley built to house her family in, the red brick boxes increasing and encroaching, the sons-in-law, all substantial men, it appeared, straining at their clothing, mopping up their gravy before they retired to the pleasures of chenille and silky oak. And the children: too good, too clean, too nice—too bad, in fact.

Nothing but faith could have resisted such very material opposition, and Miss Hare did have hers, to revive which she would run off into the bush, and after picking up the crystal thread, follow it over pebbles. Each pool would reveal its relevant mystery, of which she herself was never the least. Finally she would be renewed. Returning by a different way, she would recognize the Hand in every veined leaf, and would bundle with the bee into the divine Mouth. If she no longer raised her eyes to the evening sky, it was because she had not yet recovered all her strength. Morning is for the weaker souls; in that she walked gratefully, and not without considerable deep knowledge.

On such a morning, of confusion and solution, she found herself closer to the dark man than she had ever been before. Already she had come across this person once or twice on the roads round Sarsaparilla, although she gathered from the Godbold children that he lived somewhere at Barranugli.

He was an abo, or something, Else, the eldest Godbold, *thought*.

He could be a Syrian, or Indian, or a sort of gypsy, Gracie shouted.

Maudie yelled that Gracie did not know a thing.

Anyway, Saturday, the black got drunk, and was laying in the nettles, Kate knew for certain.

Else shushed her sister.

It was Maudie who added the only sober, factual information. He worked at the place that made the bicycle lamps, where their dad had gone for a bit, until he got fed up—Rosetree's factory, just outside of Barranugli. Maudie had seen the black knocking off along with the other men. He was carrying his tucker bag, and a big, square piece of board, she had wondered for what.

There were six Godbolds, all girls, some of whom could usually be seen in the scrub round Xanadu, lugging a puppy, or nursing a bird, and intent on business of their own. In one way and another the Godbold girls knew a lot. Their bodies and the soles of their feet were hard, and their minds, on the whole, sensible.

That they were not better informed on the subject of Miss Hare's black was rather surprising, though Miss Hare herself was not surprised, nor would she have wished it otherwise, for she respected privacy. Seldom did she meet human beings, and those she did, she would not know how to address. She preferred to peer at them through leaves, when she herself was practically reduced to light and shadow. Then, at last, she was truly in her element.

So she would peer out at her dark man on those occasions when he walked through the lanes which ran past Xanadu. Once she had entered through his eyes, and at first glance recognized familiar furniture, and once again she had entered in, and their souls had stroked each other with reassuring feathers, but very briefly, for each had suddenly taken fright. From then on, they had been inclined to avoid each other, until on that specific morning, not long after Miss Hare's trial by Mrs Jolley had begun, the dark person actually spoke.

It was like this.

Miss Hare had come out from behind a clump of eggs-and-bacon, on the edge of the scrub, at the bend in the road below Xanadu. She had come out, and was herself standing on the edge, where, she realized at once, she had been caught. For she heard feet approaching over stones. And there he was, the dark man, almost level with her.

On this occasion the stranger appeared to take their situation for granted. He was all bones, and might have seemed to shamble, if it

had not been for a certain convinced bearing. His full lips were
slightly, lazily open, on obviously excellent teeth, and his voice
sounded agreeable, direct, and unexpected. For he addressed her
immediately, as though it had always been intended that he should.

"The water," he said, and pointed, "is creeping up on you. Don't
you know it? Eh? You are standing in a bog."

Miss Hare did, then, look at her feet.

"The water," she repeated, or choked.

"In a minute you will know all about it," warned the voice. "It
will come in over the tops of your shoes."

Then he passed, and she was left standing at the roadside, where
she could recently have witnessed a procession.

Her shoes did not matter, of course. It was a mild morning, ruled
by a still air. The leaves were resting together.

As the man continued along the road, the stones were crunched
steadily, but easily beneath his feet. He was excessively thin, and
slack-bodied, but his shoulders, she saw, were at peace. At least,
for the moment. It was doubtful whether a human being, any more
than the weather, could remain permanently at rest.

She watched his back, gratefully rewarded. Both the illuminates
remained peacefully folded inside the envelopes of their flesh. Each
knew it was improbable they would ever communicate in words.
Yet, they had exchanged a token of goodness, which would remain
forever in each other's keeping. From behind closed eyelids, each
would have recognized the other as an apostle of truth. And that
was enough.

Then the water did come in over the tops of Miss Hare's shoes,
as the stranger had predicted, but she did not altogether mind, nor
did she withdraw immediately.

When she got in, Mrs Jolley had returned from church.

"Oh, the lovely hymns!" the latter exclaimed. "And the sermon!
The clergyman was lovely."

"I am glad you were satisfied," said Miss Hare.

"Religion is not a meal," protested the housekeeper.

"It is everything anyone wishes it to be."

"There are the heathens, of course. And what have you been up
to, I would like to know?"

"I have been in the bush," Miss Hare confessed.

Mrs Jolley sucked her perfect teeth.

"And on a Sunday!"

"Every day is the same," replied Miss Hare.

"But Sunday is not a day for scarecrows," Mrs Jolley could not resist.

"No," Miss Hare began, rather more timidly. "It is a day for Christians."

Mrs Jolley did not hear.

"Did you see nobody you knew?" she asked her employer, but very cold. Employer, indeed! On that wage, she was doing a favour.

"No," said Miss Hare, in a sense truthfully.

But feared for what, in truth, had also been a lie.

"That is," she corrected herself, "I saw the dark man."

"Pooh! Some dirty abo bloke! I would not have an abo come near me. And in the bush! They are all undesirable persons. And in the bush! You will run into trouble, my lady. Mark my words, if I am not right."

Though she had to smile, and not to herself.

"I am told the aboriginals *are* a very dirty lot. And drunk, and disorderly," Miss Hare had to admit.

But it was she herself who felt dirty. Mrs Jolley had dirtied her.

Mrs Jolley had hung her fur on the back of a kitchen chair. It was a silver fox, she would declare, and a present from the family. Mrs Jolley's fur was, incontestably, a reminder.

Miss Hare felt miserable.

Mrs Jolley began to know it. She yanked a pan out of a cupboard and clanked it extra hard.

"And what was the name of this abo?"

"I do not know," said Miss Hare, "but will inquire of the Godbolds, if it is of interest."

"Who are the Godbolds?"

"They are some children. Their mother is my friend."

"You don't say! You have a friend, then?"

"Yes."

"Is she a nice lady?"

"She lives in a shed below the post-office, and takes in washing."

Mrs. Jolley breathed hard.

"I would not of thought that a lady like you, of Topnotch Hall, and all, would associate beneath them. Mind you, I do not criticize.

It is not my business, is it? Only I cannot truly say I have ever been on any sort of terms with a lady living in a shed."

But by now Miss Hare was too rapt to have been acquainted with any other.

"Ah, but she," she told very humbly, "she is the best of women."

Miss Hare would remember how she used to listen for the footsteps on the stairs. Very firm, rather heavy, relentless, they had seemed, until time and familiarity drew attention to the constancy of those sounds. Soon the woman lying in the room above could barely endure the tumult of her own emotions as she waited for the door to open.

It was during a winter of the Second War that people—at least one or two of them—began to wonder what had become of that old Miss Hare. It was a harmless thought, and so, quickly dropped, until one morning, running through the frost across what had been the lawn at Xanadu, young Gracie, who, of all the Godbolds, had made that place her especial hunting ground, saw something at a window, and went and told her mum.

Although she had not seen *much,* because of the dressing-table mirror jammed against the window, she thought she had recognized a piece of old Miss Hare. And Miss Hare had looked queer. Now, Gracie Godbold had never seen a ghost, but if she had, she knew it would have looked sort of misty-dirty like.

So it was natural for the mother, a conscientious woman, to put on her hat, and sober coat, and go down to investigate.

Nobody ever heard what emotions Mrs Godbold had experienced in the rooms and on the stairs at Xanadu. Discreet by nature, she was also uncommunicative. But she did at last, by peering and calling, arrive at the cell which contained the survivor, somewhere in the centre of that vast and crumbling comb.

Miss Hare was lying on a bed of pomp and tatters.

She said, "Mrs. Godbold, is it? I have been feeling rather unwell for several days. But hope it will pass with patience. I do not believe in fussing and doctors, because, look at the animals. Oh, dear, but I become breathless, and it is terribly cold when the frost sets in."

"I see," said Mrs Godbold, and thought.

She began very soon to do things. Simple, but soothing, as accorded with her own nature. She made Miss Hare comfortable. She washed her at evening using a crystal basin the Hares had brought from Vienna—was it?—but long ago. She heated bricks and wrapped them in a blanket. And from the shed in which she lived, she brought, on that, and many evenings after, milk in a little white-enamelled can, a brown egg, and a slice or two from an enormous loaf.

So Mrs Godbold nursed Miss Hare the winter the latter had pneumonia. Many people remained unaware, because Mrs Godbold did not talk, and Godbolds were no-hopers of the worst kind, and who, anyway, ever saw or spoke with that old, dirty, mad Miss Hare?

Yet, she reappeared. She had begun, very tentative, supporting herself on the furniture, and, like a dog, listening for familiar sounds on the empty stairs.

"You see, miss," said Mrs Godbold. "Soon you will be outside again."

"Ah," said Miss Hare, "then I shall breathe."

But quickly looked at her companion's somewhat flat and pallid face.

"I shall be sorry, too," she added, "because you will come to me no more."

Mrs Godbold made a little noise that was difficult to interpret.

Then they glanced together, out of the window, at Xanadu, on which the mists had begun to hang, so that if it had not been for their own group of solid statuary, the world might have seemed at that hour ephemeral and melancholy.

For Miss Hare, Mrs Godbold had become, and indeed remained, the most positive evidence of good. Physically she was too massive, and to some, no doubt, displeasing: too coarse, too flat of face, thick-armed, big of breast, waxy-skinned, the large pores opened by the steam from her copper. But nobody could deny Mrs Godbold her breadth of brow. She wore her hair in thick and glistening coils, and her eyes were a steady grey.

As for her existence, that was endless. She knew by heart the grey hours when the world evolves, and would only rest a while to enjoy the evening star. Strangled by the arms of a weaned child, she was seldom, it seemed, without a second baby greedy at her breast, and a third impatient in her body. She would scrub, wash, bake,

mend, and drag her husband from floor to bed when, of an evening, he had fallen down.

"You will exhaust yourself," Miss Hare warned.

"I am used to it," Mrs Godbold replied. "And am strong, besides.
When I was a girl, we would work in the fields, and walk for miles.
That was in the fens. Before I came out. Flat country, certainly, but
it does not let you eat it up all that easy." She laughed. "We would
skate, too, all of us girls and boys; we was nine in the family. We
would skate across the flooded country during a hard winter, miles
and miles, everything so brittle. The twigs on the hedges looked as
if you could have broken them off like glass."

Her eyes were suddenly brightened by what she was telling.
Solidity in herself seemed to give to the glass twigs some mysterious,
desirable, unattainable property of their own.

Once while Miss Hare was feverish, and really very ill, she confided in her nurse, "I am afraid I may fall and hurt myself on so
much glass. Will you let me hold your hand?"

"Yes," agreed the other, and gave it.

She might have severed it, if necessary, with its wedding ring
and all.

"Gold," Miss Hare mumbled. "Champing at the bit. Did you
ever see the horses? I haven't yet. But at times, the wheels crush
me unbearably."

Mrs Godbold remained a seated statue. The massive rumps of
her horses waited, swishing their tails through eternity. The wheels
of her chariot were solid gold, well-axled, as might have been expected. Or so it seemed to the sick woman, whose own vision never
formed, remaining a confusion of light, at most an outline of vague
and fiery pain.

"Never," complained Miss Hare. "Never. Never. As if I were not
intended to discover."

Whereupon she succeeded in twisting herself upright.

"Go to sleep. Too much talk will not do you any good," advised
the nurse.

And looked put out, at least for her, as if the patient had destroyed something they had been sharing.

"Oh, but I am ill," Miss Hare whimpered.

Mrs Godbold let the silence slip by. Then, ever so gradually, she
had ventured on a suggestion.

"I will pray for you," she said.

"If it will do you any good," Miss Hare sighed. "I hope you will take the opportunity. But leaves are best, I find, plastered moist on the forehead."

Then she drifted off, and Mrs Godbold continued to sit beside her for a while. Evening was a perfect silence. The tranquil light, interceding with the darkness, held for a moment a thread of cobweb in its balance.

When she was recovered, Miss Hare decided on one occasion to sound her friend.

"I believe we exchanged some confidences while I was so ill."

Mrs Godbold did not wish to answer, but felt compelled to.

"What confidences?" she asked, turning away.

"About the Chariot."

Mrs Godbold blushed.

"Some people," she said, "get funny ideas when they are sick."

Miss Hare was not deceived, however, and remained convinced they would continue to share a secret, after her friend had returned to carry out her life sentence of love and labour in the shed below the post-office.

That some secret did exist, Mrs Jolley also was certain, with her instinct for doors through which she might never be admitted. Not that she wanted to be. Oh dear, no, not for a moment.

"Sounds a peculiar person to me," she had to comment, when her employer had concluded the story of her illness, or such parts of it as were communicable.

Miss Hare laughed. Her face was quite transformed.

Mrs Jolley swelled, only just perceptibly.

"And what will become of her," she asked, "in that shed, with all those children, and the husband—what about the husband?"

Had she put her finger on a sore?

"Oh, the husband comes and goes. On several occasions he has hit her, and once he loosened several of her teeth. He has been in prison, you know, for drunkenness.

"Oh, yes, the husband!" she was forced to add.

And she began to sway her head from side to side, in a manner both troubled and grotesque, which gave her companion considerable satisfaction.

"There is so much evil," finally cried the distraught Miss Hare. "One forgets."

"I can never forget," Mrs Jolley claimed. "It is always with us, in the daily papers, not to mention the back yard."

"I had forgotten," Miss Hare realized, "until *you* reminded me of it."

"But," said Mrs Jolley, doing something dainty with a white of egg, "why doesn't she leave this husband?"

"She considers it her duty to stay with him. Besides, she loves him."

Miss Hare pronounced with difficulty that amazing word.

"One day, on my way past, I shall give her a piece of advice."

"You would not dare!" cried Miss Hare, protecting something breakable. "She is a very sensitive woman," she said.

"Squeezing the water out of sheets!" retorted Mrs Jolley.

Then Miss Hare suspected that her housekeeper might ultimately have everybody at her mercy.

"Nobody who is a believer could fail to derive consolation from her faith," Mrs Jolley decided.

"Few could fail to believe in Mrs Godbold," Miss Hare followed up.

But feebler. Mrs Jolley had experience of words. Mrs Jolley had her family in a phalanx, her three daughters, and her sons-in-law, to say nothing of the incalculable kiddies.

"None of all this," said Mrs Jolley at last, "is what I am used to. I have always moved in different circles."

Miss Hare believed it, but also feared.

"Mrs Flack agrees," said Mrs Jolley, "that I have been faced with things recently which I cannot be expected to understand or accept."

"Mrs Flack?"

"Mrs Flack is a friend," said Mrs Jolley, and let fall a veil of sugar from her sifter. "A lady," she said, "that I met on the bus. And again, outside the church. The widow," she added, "of a tiler, who fell off the roof while contracted at Barranugli, years ago."

"I have never heard of Mrs Flack."

"Different circumstances," continued Mrs Jolley, with dignity, if not scorn. "Mrs Flack resides in Mildred Street, in a home of her own, with every amenity. Seeing as her husband, the tiler, had the trade connections that he had, they were able to fix things real nice. Oh, and I almost forgot to tell: Mrs Flack's father was a wealthy store proprietor, who saw to it, naturally, that his daughter was left comfortable."

"Naturally," Miss Hare agreed.

Expected to evoke for herself the apparition of Mrs Flack, her mind would not venture so far. And there the name rested, unspoken and mysterious.

Indeed, Mrs Jolley, too, became a mystery now. She would appear in doorways, or from behind dividing curtains, and cough, but very carefully, at certain times. She carried her eyes downcast. Or she would raise them. And look. And Mrs Jolley's eyes were blue.

"I was looking for the ashtrays," Mrs Jolley would explain. "All my girls are smokers, of course. And the trays need emptying."

Then she would retire. She was most discreet now, and silent.

Again she would appear.

"Do you need anything?" Mrs Jolley would ask, or breathe.

What can one possibly need? Miss Hare used to wonder.

"No," she would have to confess.

She would go on sitting in her favourite chair, which was old, but real.

"Some people are given to one thing, and some another," Mrs Jolley would say, and finger. "Now, *we* have the Genoa velvets in all our lounges. But Mrs Flack—the lady I was telling you of— she goes for *petty point*."

But Mrs Flack would at once withdraw.

"Do you need anything?" Mrs Jolley would repeat.

Miss Hare's face fumbled after some acceptable desire.

"No," she would have to admit, ashamed.

Then, on one occasion, Mrs Jolley announced, "I had a letter."

She had followed her employer out to the terrace. It was almost evening. Great cloudy tumbrils were lumbering across the bumpy sky towards a crimson doom.

"I did not see your letter," Miss Hare replied.

Mrs Jolley scarcely hesitated.

"Oh," she said, "it was at the P.O. All my correspondence is always directed to the P.O. A matter of policy, you might say."

Miss Hare was observing the progress of a beetle across the mouth of a silted urn. She would have much preferred not to be disturbed.

"It was a letter from Mrs Apps," Mrs Jolley pursued. "That is Merle, the eldest. Merle has a particular weakness for her mum, perhaps because she was delicate as a kiddy. But struck lucky later on. With a hubby who denies her nothing—within reason, of course, and the demands of his career. Mr Apps—his long service will soon be due—is an executive official at the Customs. I will not say well-thought-of. Indispensable is nearer the mark. So it is not uncommon for Merle to hobnob with the high-ups of the Service, and entertain them to a buffy at her home. *Croaky de poison.* Chipperlarters. All that. With perhaps a substantial dish of, say, chicken à la king. I never believe in blowing my own horn, but Merle does things that lovely. Yes. Her buffy has been written up, not once but several times."

Miss Hare observed her beetle.

"Now Merle writes," the housekeeper continued, "and does not, well, exactly *say,* because Merle is never one to *say,* but lets it be understood she is not at all satisfied with the steps her mum has taken to lead an independent life, since their father passed on, like that, so tragically."

Mrs. Jolley watched Miss Hare.

"Of course I did not tell her half. Because Merle would have created. But you will realize the position it has put me in. Seeing as I am a person that always sympathizes with the misfortunes of others."

Mrs Jolley watched Miss Hare. The wind had started up, and the housekeeper did not like it in the open. She was one who would walk very quickly along a road, and hope to reach the shops.

"Everybody is unfortunate, if you can recognize it," said Miss Hare, helping her beetle. "But there are usually compensations for misfortune."

Mrs Jolley drew in her breath. She hated it on the horrid terrace, the wind tweaking her hair-net, and the smell of night threatening her.   .

"At a nominal wage," she protested, "it is hard lines if a lady should have to look for compensations."

"How people can talk!" Miss Hare exclaimed, not without admiration. "My parents would be at it by the hour. But one could sit quite comfortably inside their words. In a kind of tent. Do you know? When it rains."

"Your parents, poor souls!" Mrs Jolley could not resist.

So that Miss Hare was cut. She removed her finger from the beetle, which ultimately she could not assist.

"Why must you keep harping on my parents?"

The marbled sky was heartrending, if also adamant, its layers of mauve and rose veined by now with black and indigo. The moon was the pale fossil of a moth.

"Who brought them up?" Mrs Jolley laughed against the rather nasty wind. "I have always had consideration for Somebody's feelings, particularly since Somebody witnessed such a very peculiar death."

Miss Hare was almost turned to stone, amongst the neglected urns and the Diana—*Scuola Canova*—whose hand had been broken off at the wrist.

"Will you, please, leave me?" she asked.

"That is what I have been trying to convey," insisted Mrs Jolley. "No person can be put upon indefinitely. And I have been invited," she said, "or it has been suggested by a friend, who suffers from indifferent health, that I should keep her company."

Miss Hare was gulping like a brown frog. It was not the eventuality that appalled, so much as the method of disclosure, and the shock.

"Then, if you really intend," she mumbled.

Mrs Jolley could have devoured one whom she suspected of a weakness.

"It is not as if you wasn't independent before," she reminded, and smiled. "We could hardly call ourselves Australians—could we?— if we was not independent. There is none of my girls as is not able, at a pinch, to mend a fuse, paint the home, or tackle jobs of carpentry."

Mrs Jolley had assumed that monumental stance of somebody with whom it is impossible to argue.

"Perhaps," Miss Hare answered.

When all was said, she would remain a sandy little girl. Her smiles would weave like shallow water over pebbles.

"So," sighed Mrs Jolley, "there it is. I cannot say any more. Nothing stands still, and we must go along too."

Then she drew in her breath, as if she were restraining wind.

Or else she could suddenly have been afraid.

"Do let go of me, please!" she said, rather loud, but still controlled.

"Miss Hare!" she said, louder. "You are hurting my wrists!"

But Miss Hare, for her part, could not resist the black gusts of darkness that were bearing down on her, and if she did not know the satisfaction of recognizing Mrs Jolley's fear, it was because she became engulfed in her own; she was removed from herself, at least temporarily, at that point.

As for Mrs Jolley, night had closed on her like a vise, leaving her just freedom enough to wrestle with the serpents of her conscience. So the two women were thrashing it out on the gritty terrace. The wind, or something, had torn the housekeeper's hair-net, and she hissed, or cried, from between her phosphorescent teeth.

Several afternoons a week, after putting on her gloves, and hat with eye-veil, Mrs Jolley would not exactly go, she would *proceed,* rather, to her friend's residence at Sarsaparilla. Up the hill and into the street, it was not far, but far enough to turn a walk into a mission. How much solider a pavement sounded. Mrs Jolley would stamp and kick until she felt satisfied. The mere sight of a bus passing through a built-up area restored a person's circulation, as rounds of beef and honeycombs of tripe fed the spirit, and ironmongery touched the heart. So Mrs Jolley would continue on her way, under the lophostemons, as far as Mildred Street. Five minutes from the Cash-and-Carry, with doctor handy on the corner, it was a most desirable address. So Mrs Jolley would proceed, smiling at the ladies in the windows of their brick homes. She might correct the position of a seam or two. Then she would be ready to arrive.

If Mrs Flack's brick looked best of all, her tiles better, brighter-glazed, it was perhaps because of her late husband's connections with the trade. There KARMA stood, the name done in baked enamel. Considering the delicate state of her health, the owner risked too much for neatness, though certainly she paid an elderly man a few shillings to mow the grass, and had almost succeeded in encouraging an older one to do the same for less. On Thursdays, besides, a strong woman coped with any stooping or lifting, but that arrangement might possibly be discontinued. Depending on developments.

Mrs Jolley loved the latch at Mrs Flack's. She loved the rustic picket gate. She loved the hedge of Orange Triumph. To run her glove along the surface of Mrs Flack's brick home gave her shivers. The sound of its convenience swept her head over heels into the caverns of envy.

As for Mrs Flack herself, she would seldom greet her friend with more than: "Hmmmm!"

Or: "Well I never!"

Or, at most: "I did not look at the calendar, but might have known."

Yet Mrs Jolley understood the significance of it all. She might have been a cat, except that she was rubbing on the air.

Mrs Flack was sometimes described as having rather a yellow look, although, more accurately speaking, she was a medium shade of buff. For many years, she told, she had suffered from derangement of the bile. She was the victim of gallstones, too, and varicose veins, to say nothing of her Heart. She was wedded to her Heart, it might have seemed, if it had not been known she was a widow. Yet, in spite of such complications and allegiances, she would get about in a slow, definite way, and even when she had not been there, was remarkably well informed on everything that had happened. Indeed, it had been suggested by those few who were lacking in respect that Mrs Flack was omnipresent—under the beds, even, along with the fluff and the chamber-pots. But most people had too much respect for her presence to question her authority. Her hats were too sober, her reports too factual. Where flippancy is absent, truth can only be inferred, and her teeth were broad and real enough to lend additional weight and awfulness to words.

Remarks collapsed on Mrs Jolley's lips in the presence of her friend. *Her friend.* The word was quite alarming, if also magical. Mrs Flack would look up from lashing the Orange Triumphs with the jet from her plastic hose, or, seated in her own lounge, behind a prophetic steam of tea, would simply look, before pronouncing.

"That poor soul," she might begin, "who we both know—there is no need to mention names—how she has survived all these years on a slice of bread and dripping, and her relatives well-to-do, not to say downright wealthy. They did, for their own convenience, after the death of the mother, deliver her to an institution, but the person screamed and screamed, and clung to the railings with her two hands, so that they were forced to take her back. It only goes to show. I am always thankful that, in my case, there are no ties, no encumbrances, not even a mortgage on the home."

"Ah," Mrs Jolley had to protest, "I am a mother!"

Mrs Flack would pause, pick a burnt currant from a scone, and appear to accuse it terribly.

"I cannot claim any such experience," she would declare.

Then, after frowning, she would fall to laughing, but feebly— she was an invalid, it had to be remembered—through strips of pale lips.

Like cheese-straws at a buffy, Mrs Jolley would be reminded, and immediately regret her disrespect.

"I did not mean," she would hasten, dashing at a few crumbs. "That is to say, I did not intend to suggest." And then: "Are you truly quite alone?"

"Yes, dear." Mrs Flack would sigh.

At that moment something would happen, of such peculiar subtlety that it must have eluded the perception of all but those involved in the experience. The catalyst of sympathy seemed to destroy the envelopes of personality, leaving the two essential beings free to merge and float. Thought must have played little part in any state so passive, so directionless, yet it was difficult not to associate a mental process with silence of such a ruthless and pervasive kind. As they continued sitting, the two women would drench the room with the moth-colours of their one mind. Little sighs would break, scintillating, on the Wilton wall-to-wall. The sound of stomachs, rumbling liquidly, would sluice the already impeccable veneer. Glances rejected one another as obsolete aids to communication. This could have been the perfect communion of souls, if, at the same time, it had not suggested perfect collusion.

Mrs Jolley was usually the first to return. Certain images would refurnish the swept chamber of her mind. There was, for instance —she loved it best of all—the pastel blue plastic dressing-table set in Mrs Flack's second bedroom.

Mrs Jolley's face would grow quite hard and lined then, as if a pink-and-blue eiderdown had suffered petrifaction.

"Alone perhaps, but in a lovely home," she would be heard to murmur.

"Alone is not the same," Mrs Flack would usually reply.

And smile.

It was not all that sad. They both knew it was not sad. They understood that a dénouement might be reached in the drama of their wishes—if they so wished.

As tea and contentment increased understanding of each other, as well as confidence in their own powers, it was only to be expected that two ladies of discretion and taste should produce their knives and try them for sharpness on weaker mortals. Seated above the world on springs and *petty point,* they could lift the lids and look right into the boxes in which moiled other men, crack open craniums as if they had been boiled eggs, read letters before they had been written, scent secrets that would become a source of fear to those concerned. Eventually the ladies would begin. Their methods would be steel, though their antiphon was always bronze.

"Take doctors, for instance," Mrs Flack might say. "Doctors are only human beings."

"You are telling me!" it was Mrs Jolley's duty to interpose.

"But must be expected to act different."

"And do not always."

"Very often do not. Mrs Jolley, I am telling you that this doctor at the corner, in giving me a needle—which I have to get regular, for certain reasons—pulled me quite close. 'Is it necessary?' I asked —myself, of course—'and according to medical etiquette, to press against a lady's form in giving her a simple needle?' His breath was that hot, Mrs Jolley, and the odour, well, I am not one to insinuate, but if it had been *my* breath, I would of been ashamed to advertise the fact."

"Ttst, ttst! The doctors! And to think that a lady, on some occasions, must submit to an examination by such hands!"

"Ho, an examination! I have never had one, and do not intend to. No, never!"

"There are the lady doctors, of course."

"Ah, the lady doctors!"

"Do you suppose the lady doctors ever attend to gentlemen?"

"I do not know. But they would not attend to me, never. I have my own ideas about the lady doctors."

Mrs Jolley would have liked to hear, but etiquette did not permit.

"Ah, yes." Mrs Flack would sigh, and lapse.

Though each knew she must soon revive. It was but the pause between movements, when initiates clear their throats and frown at some innocent who gives expression to his pleasure. Mrs Jolley had quickly learnt.

"Thursday night"—Mrs Flack had, indeed, revived—"Mrs Khalil's Lurleen was seen three times outside the Methodist church."

"In the open?"

"On the grass."

"Accompanied?"

"Ho! Mrs Khalil's Lurleen!"

"But with a gentleman?"

"With three. And all of them different. Between the pictures' going in and coming out."

Then Mrs Jolley had to laugh.

"Girls will be girls, eh?"

"I should hope not," said Mrs Flack, whose pale lips would become transformed at times into two strips of adhesive tape. "Such girls should be run out. But when the law—well, what can you expect at Sarsaparilla?"

"Did you say the law?"

"I will not go into that," Mrs Flack replied. "Except that the constable's own braces was found in the paddy's lucerne on the block below the pictures. There is no denying ownership when the name is put in marking-ink."

"He could have lost them."

"He could have lost them."

"Or thrown them away."

"Or thrown them away. With the price still visible on the brand-new leather. No, Mrs Jolley, Constable McFaggott is far too close to lose or discard his belongings in the paddy's lucerne, unless the duty that took him there had turned him lighter-headed than usual."

Then Mrs Jolley began to hiss like any goose. Her pink-and-blue was changed to purple.

"What do you know!" She sat and hissed, and would have known more.

But Mrs Flack had folded her arms. She was holding the blanched points of her yellow elbows.

"We have not kept to the subject," she said, or accused.

For Mrs Flack could sense with only half her instinct that her friend had something which she wished to tell.

The occasion was, in fact, the day after Mrs Jolley had approached her mistress on the terrace and been involved in something rather nasty. How nasty, the housekeeper scarcely dared remember. But would touch her wrists from time to time. Certainly, on setting out, so brisk and bright, on the visit to her friend, she had fully intended to confide, perhaps even make the great decision. Yet, could she, finally? Or would she?

"That poor soul at Xanadu," Mrs Flack had begun to lead, "I do feel sorry for the sick and simple."

"But in her case, has had her day."

"There are all kinds, I must admit."

"But has had her day, Mrs Flack. All that lot has had their day."

Mrs Jolley could not pass her tongue quick enough along her stripped lips, nor twist her nice openwork gloves into a tight enough knot.

Mrs Flack's eyes began to dart, so that her friend was unpleasantly reminded that somebody was behind the skin.

"We must think of ourselves as well, of course," Mrs Flack agreed.

"We must think of ourselves."

"Without killing *her!*"

"Not likely!" Mrs Jolley laughed. "She must run the risk, though. Like any girl in a kennel beneath the roof. When the heat used to crack. Or shelling peas. Or pushing the pea-pods through the sieve. Or blacking the grates. Or blacking the grates."

"Are you bitter, Mrs Jolley?"

"Bitter, no. I am just remembering."

"One thing I never was, was bitter," Mrs Flack announced.

Then they sat for a moment, to experience once again that delicious process of disembodiment and union.

But time was passing. Mrs Jolley got up, brisk, good body that she was, and slapped her dainty gloves together.

"Well," she said, "it has been lovely, Mrs Flack. And now I must get back to that poor lady of mine."

And sniffed, and smiled, and blinked at once.

At which her friend became her most dignified and formal. The classic gestures might have been detached from a frieze.

"If you was ever to decide, we would consider this as *your* chair," said Mrs Flack, laying two fingers and a ruby ring on an excessive bulge in the upholstery.

Mrs Jolley could not bring herself to look, let alone comment. But the implications were understood.

"It was the one He used to sit in, after an early tea," on this occasion Mrs Flack went so far as to confide. "He liked his comfort, and an early tea. No one else will never ever have the use of that chair, without it is a certain trusted friend."

Yet, Mrs Jolley had become far too agitated to decide. Her mouth, her gestures were unlike themselves. Two masters could have been contending for the strings.

She was forced to reply, "I am expecting a letter that will help me give a straight answer on the future. You know how it is."

"Only the person herself knows how it is," Mrs Flack said, and smiled.

In the hands of Fate, and exhausted by conflict, Mrs Jolley held her head humbly and acceptant. She allowed herself to be led along the hall, past "The Two Little Princesses with Their Dogs," and a bloodhound that Mrs Flack herself had worked in wool while waiting for her late husband to propose.

The two ladies seldom continued their conversation at parting, unless to consider briefly the prospects for rain or fine, and soon Mrs Jolley would be going down the street, still holding her head in a chastened way, like a communicant returning from the altar, conscious that all the ladies, in all the windows, of all the homes, were aware of her shriven state. For, there was no doubt, friendship did purify.

Although there was no more mention of Mrs Flack, she was always there at Xanadu. Miss Hare could feel her presence. In certain rather metallic light, behind clumps of ragged, droughty laurels, in corners of rooms where dry rot had encouraged the castors to burst through the boards, on landings where wallpaper hung in drunken, brown festoons, or departed from the wall in one long, limp sheet Mrs Flack obtruded worst, until Miss Hare began to fear, not only for her companion and housekeeper, at the best of times a doubtful asset, but, what was far more serious, for the safety of her property. So far had Mrs Flack, through the medium of Mrs Jolley, insinuated herself into the cracks in the actual stone. Sometimes the owner of Xanadu would wake in her lumpy bed, and listen for the crash. Or would there be a mere dull, tremendous flump, as quantities of passive dust subsided?

Either eventuality terrified Miss Hare.

One night she got the hiccups, and the marble halls of Xanadu reverberated with the same distress. Glass tinkled as she wandered here and there, grazing with an arm or elbow. Lustre crashed somewhere in the drawing-room.

"What are you up to, clumsy girl?" Mrs Jolley called. "Can't I leave you for two minutes?"

Already she was coming. Mrs Jolley would appear at crucial moments, now from above, it seemed, her detached soles smacking marble. She was carrying a lamp, which flew through the darkness like a small bouquet of flowers. Mrs Jolley stood at last in the drawing-room holding her bunch of yellow flowers.

"You are not to be trusted, you know," said the reliable housekeeper, catching sight of the glittery fragments of the silver-lustre jug.

"Aren't they my own things?" the owner dared.

"Oh, yes!" The housekeeper laughed. "They are your own things all right."

"And no one will take them from me?"

"Not till you have smashed them all to smithereens. Home, too, it looks like. What will you do then? Camp out under the bunya-bunya, and count the raindrops?"

"I have the hiccups," said Miss Hare. "Or had, rather. I believe they have been cured."

Mrs Jolley's little yellow bouquet shook.

"It was the fright you got. You could set up and make your fortune, throwing junk at all the hiccuppers in creation."

The darkness was reeling under the attacks of Mrs Jolley's mirth. Miss Hare, although cured of her hiccups, felt quite sick.

"Mrs Jolley," she began, "your *friend* . . ."

The formidable word seemed to thunder.

But Mrs Jolley, wheezing inside her iron corset, had bent to retrieve the fragments of jug, and was making an icy music with them, as she swept them together over the floor. It was probable she had not heard the word. Nor did Miss Hare know how she would have continued if her housekeeper had.

For, although Mrs Flack pervaded, she was nothing tangible.

Then Mrs Jolley straightened up.

"You will not leave me?" Miss Hare asked.

The woman stood. It was as if she had discovered a swelling on her lip. It was most embarrassing.

"In the dark, I mean," Miss Hare explained.

"You was here before, wasn't you?" Now Mrs Jolley's voice quite clattered. "Having the hiccups. And before that. And before that."

She appeared annoyed.

"Oh, yes," said Miss Hare. "And shall be. If I am allowed. I shall throw back the shutter. I had forgotten the moon. I shall sit for a little. Quietly."

Soon there were a few planks of moonlight, in which she continued to rock long after Mrs Jolley had withdrawn. For much longer than she had anticipated, the wanderer kept afloat, and by extraordinary managment of the will always just avoided bumping against the shores of darkness. Other shapes threatened, though, some of them dissolving at the last moment into good, some she was able to identify unhesitatingly as evil. In the misty silence, the two women, her tormentors-in-chief, let down their hair and covered their faces with veils of it. Their words were hidden from her. On the whole, she realized, she was unable to distinguish motives unless allowed to read faces.

Towards morning Mrs Jolley appeared in the flesh and wrenched the little tiller from the cold hands. As she joggled the boat in anger, dewdrops fell distinctly from all its protruberances.

"You do hate me," said Miss Hare, observing evil in person.

The rescuer's face was quivering with exasperation. The mouth had aged without its teeth, and should have proclaimed innocence, but words flickered almost lividly from between the gums.

"I am only thinking of your health," Mrs Jolley hissed. "I am responsible in a way, though do not know what possessed me to take it on."

Then evil is also good, Miss Hare understood.

"But you have not yet enjoyed all the pleasure of tormenting me," she was moved to remark.

"I will not waste my breath arguing with loopy Louie," replied Mrs Jolley, leading her charge towards the stairs.

At breakfast each of them treated the incident as if it had not occurred. It was a brisk morning. It seemed to Miss Hare that the light illuminated. She herself was exuberant with knowledge. She radiated discoveries.

"I see," she said, over the crispies, "I am wrong about Xanadu. To be afraid. I shall not fear if it is taken away, because my experience will remain."

"Experience!" exploded Mrs Jolley. "What have *you* experienced?"

"For many years, when there were people here, I sat under the table, amongst the legs, and saw an awful lot happen."

"There's always plenty happens in a big house, but it's only the servants that sees that. You were sitting on the same cushions as your mum and dad."

"I was the servant of the servants. I was a very ugly little girl. The maids would read me their letters, because I hardly existed, and sometimes would allow me to fetch them things, especially before they were going out, in their big pink hats, to meet their friends."

Mrs Jolley breathed on nonsense.

"Better eat up your crispies," she advised.

"But that is not the experience of which I wish to speak. Take water, for instance. If you are alone with it enough, you become like water. You enter into it."

Mrs Jolley had got up and was throwing the crockery into the sink. The plates were falling dangerously hard, but somehow failed to break.

"Whether this can count as my contribution," Miss Hare continued, "I still have to discover. Perhaps somebody will tell me. And show me at the same time how to distinguish with certainty between good and evil."

Mrs Jolley's face, which was still eating, had become a series of lumps. Obviously she was not going to answer, and it was not only because her mouth was full.

"For all I know, Xanadu, which I still can't help love, is evil itself."

"It is that all right!" cried Mrs Jolley, gulping the rest of the crust that had been giving trouble.

"Like certain things made of plastic," Miss Hare added. "Plastic is bad, bad!"

Now she felt definitely stronger, and Mrs Jolley was resenting it. Soon afterwards the seeker went outside, temporarily fortified by her knowledge. Of course, she realized, too, the sad extent of her shortcomings, which were tingling, as always, in her fingertips.

It was only natural, and soon became evident, that Mrs Jolley was preparing something, or a whole series of torments, as she ticked off the days. The housekeeper would stand for whole minutes in front of a calendar she had got from a grocer to rectify a deficiency, for Miss Hare herself had never stopped to think about time, let alone the days.

"Who would ever have thought I had been here all that long," the housekeeper once remarked aloud.

"*I* should have thought!" Miss Hare laughed. "But it is none the less surprising."

"It is because I have a conscience," Mrs Jolley hinted.

"I dare say it is," replied Miss Hare.

"And am waiting for guidance."

"I would guide you if I could," said Miss Hare, quite sincerely. "But you cannot tell other people."

Then Mrs Jolley stirred up the dust, as she did frequently—her conscience made her—while achieving nothing by the act.

"You know," said Miss Hare, "I think I am now strong enough if you decide to go to your friend."

Mrs Jolley was all murmurs.

Friendship, she said, sometimes involved a plunge.

"Friendship is two knives," said Miss Hare. "They will sharpen each other when rubbed together, but often one of them will slip, and slice off a thumb."

At that point Mrs Jolley flew into such a rage she tore down a curtain in the dining-room, and Miss Hare no longer minded. She sensed that for the moment she had the upper hand. Or was it that she, too, contained something evil which could take control at times? Some human element. Now she recalled, with nostalgia, occasions when she had lost her identity in those of trees, bushes, inanimate objects, or entered into the minds of animals, of which the desires were unequivocal, or honest.

Depressed, if also enlightened, she was not altogether surprised at the incident by which Mrs Jolley became reinstated in her own esteem.

One morning, rather fresh, because still early, the housekeeper had gone out into the yard, and was stamping about too much and too long to satisfy the listener. The latter was standing in a little scullery, in one corner of which she was able normally to feel at peace, in a scent of apples, sometimes a squeaking of mice, and always the broken light from an old, bulging cane blind. But on the present occasion her heart was dealing her blows as she listened to the dubious activities in the yard, and at last, clearly and unmistakably, the scrape of a spade over stone sent her rushing, tumbling, down short but sudden flights of steps, over interminable flags, past the smell of stale water, until she arrived ungainly and ashamed in the doorway which gave access to the yard.

"Ah," she cried at once, "you have killed it!"

What survived of her voice rasped her throat cruelly, and surprised the brash air of morning.

"I'll say!" Mrs Jolley blurted.

She was completely out of place in the yard, and knew it. Her hair had escaped into tails, her decent dress was disarranged, but the unusualness of the situation, together with her own inspired bravery, made her enjoy dislocation. Her smile, which should have appeared fiendish, was agreeable and innocent, as she stood looking down at the spade.

Or snake. Of which the halves were still twitching.

"You killed it!" Miss Hare protested and mourned. "I used to put out milk, and it would drink, and sometimes allow me to stand by, but I never quite succeeded in winning its confidence. There is something wrong with me," she said.

Panting.

"And so you killed the snake."

"That is not killing," said Mrs Jolley, propping the spade. "That is ridding the world of something bad."

"Who is to decide what is bad?" asked Miss Hare.

At least she had been given the strength to bear what had happened, and in the yard—where so much else had taken place: the sacrifice of her poor goat, to say nothing of her father's unmentionable end.

She stooped to pick up the limp pieces of snake.

Mrs Jolley began to shriek and hold her hair.

"It will bite you!" she cried. "They say their bite stays with them."

Miss Hare's freckled, horrible hands looked so tender and ludicrous.

Mrs Jolley fell to snickering, then to giggling.

"Brave me!" She tittered. "How did I do it?"

Nor did she watch to see how her employer disposed of the corpse. She was exhausted by her triumph.

But, almost at once, began sulking again.

Mrs Jolley would sulk for days, even forgetting she was a lady and a mother, until Miss Hare was tempted to ask, "Does Elma believe in plastic?"

Or she would beg, "Tell me about the time, Mrs Jolley, that Merle gave the buffy for the high-up officials from the Customs, and the white sauce got burnt."

She was truly interested, and would have loved also to see the officials sitting at their varnished desks during the hours of business, drinking milky tea.

Or she would ask, "You have never told me—does Mr Apps wear a moustache?"

Or: "I wonder whether I should be afraid to meet a stoker?"

Mrs Jolley would not answer, because she was sulking, and Miss Hare was half ashamed for her own powers of emulating the cruelty of human beings.

"It is I who am bad," she sighed half aloud.

All the time the house was full of reverberations. The wind would tear through it when the women forgot to close the shutters, which was almost always now, with the result that leaves had begun to litter the brocade, and once the lunch-wrap of a picnicker or commercial traveller was found in an épergne. If it had not been for her stereoscopic memories, Miss Hare would have felt surprised and pained.

Mrs Jolley said, "It is too much for me."

As for the blowing paper, it was possible to roll that into a ball, which Miss Hare did, and threw it where it would not be seen.

But all the time, it was obvious something must happen. Mrs Jolley was waiting for inspiration, Miss Hare for explanation, and to those who wait, it usually comes, in some form or another.

In the housekeeper's case, it could have been that continued absence of material symbols had shaken her religious faith, thus causing a delay. Was it possible that the piles of purple brick to which she had been used to cling were as liable to crumble as the stones of Xanadu? This was too large, too unbelievable a bomb to receive into the ordered mind, and she thrust the possibility away from her. But bombs *are* unbelievable until they actually fall. Whether Mrs Jolley suspected this, or not, behind the trembling veil of her beliefs, she would open her prayer-book and search in vain for some efficacious prayer she might have overlooked. She would even invoke the image of her late husband, until remembering certain aspects of their leave-taking: an eyebrow which had stuck, the mouth biting on a last word, forever, as if it were a stone. Then she would stop. She developed heartburn, and sometimes her teeth would remain whole mornings in the tumbler.

But, of course, the real cause of Mrs Jolley's distress was her employer. Once this was realized, Miss Hare had to suffer.

The housekeeper walked about the house humming with intentions. Doors which she had never yet opened, she now tried, and, in the course of it all, climbed to the little dome in amethyst glass, under which she found airlessness and a quantity of old chicken bones. She was always ferreting into wardrobes, through forests of long, embroidered garments, in which the cold rain of metal beads would drizzle on the backs of her hands, and tendrils of feather and drifts of down, overlooked by nesting mice, revolt her nostrils. She had forced locks, when necessary, to interpret the letters stuffed inside a drawer, but never found more than words.

In the absence of a real weapon, loaded with infallible lead, or furnished with a knife which would finish cleanly, yet cruelly, she was becoming truly desperate. It was not possible that such tunnels of decayed magnificence should lead only to an innocent and empty arena. Faced with this ultimate suspicion, Mrs Jolley was standing one morning beside the buhl table, upon which she suddenly noticed—it might always have been there, but her preoccupation could have caused her to overlook it—the fan tipped with flamingo feather, a present from the Armenian merchant in the hotel at Aswan. Mrs Jolley had barely opened the fan, a poor thing of broken tortoise-shell and tattered parchment, the feathers themselves deadened by the years, no longer flaming. She was standing, the fan half open, like her mind.

When Miss Hare realized only too clearly.

The latter had appeared in the doorway in her eternal wicker hat. That Mrs Jolley had discovered Mrs Hare's fan was in itself insignificant; the mother's relationship with her child had been one of duty rather than love. But now the daughter saw that the fan could be a hinge on which something might depend, opening out immeasurably.

"I wish you would put it down," she suggested. "It is old and very fragile."

"It is a lovely fan," Mrs Jolley simpered.

Through her half-opened mind, she appeared half devilish, half girlish.

"To carry at a ball," she added.

Memories of occasions when she had offered trayfuls of ices to dancers spun garishly.

"I do ask you to put it down," Miss Hare begged, without hope.

"How they danced in their swansdown"—Mrs Jolley laughed—"till the moths got into it. All night, and into the morning."

Then a terrible thing happened. Mrs Jolley began to dance, slowly at first, tentatively, sliding her practical work-shoes across the floor of the drawing-room at Xanadu. Her face was still only trying expressions, her arms and her body positions. But courage, or her daemon, prevailed. The muscles of her cheeks no longer twitched. Her mouth became fixed in the china smile of obsession, bluish-white. She was sliding and gliding, creaking, certainly—it could not have been otherwise in such a carapace—but borne along out of reach, or control, her own, or her employer's.

Her *employer!* It had always made her laugh. More than ever now.

Sliding and gliding, out of the drawing-room, into the dining-room. Even whirling.

Mrs Jolley threw back her head. Her throat was taut. The laughter rose up through it, to be expelled in solid lumps.

"At the ball! At the ball!" Mrs Jolley sang.

And cracked. Whirling, and coughing. It was the dust.

"However much you intend to hurt me, I shall not be hurt," Miss Hare called. "I shall not watch."

But followed after—or could she have been leading?—in her wicker hat. She was trundling and stumbling, on her short, blunt legs.

"All the young men were forever persisting," Mrs Jolley chanted, "to dance with the daughter of Xanadu."

At the same time, she made a play, with her fan, with her eyes, which had grown too young for mercy: the blue eyes of future mothers.

"All the young men with moustaches, and the smooth ones, too." How she shrieked. "And the limp cousins!

"Oh, dear!" panted Mrs Jolley.

A tuft of flamingo flew out of the fan.

Miss Hare followed. Or was she leading? In either case, she trundled. And whimpered.

The figures of the dance, though developed deviously, through room and anteroom, along passages, across landings, and up the dangerous flights of stairs, led directly into the past, and this had never seemed more grotesque, draped with calico, and dry with rouge. As Miss Hare followed—or led—and Mrs Jolley danced, sometimes obscenely moulded to a partner's chest, sometimes compelling a gilded chair to execute a teetering step, all the dancers of all the waltzes returned to Xanadu: the grave bosoms and the little pippins, the veins of coral and of watered ink, the chalk cheeks and the tortured mops, and the gentlemen, the gentlemen. Never had the ache of patent leather been admitted to such an extent as on the occasion of Mrs Jolley's lethal performance. Never had the music from Sydney broken more brilliantly under the chandelier. Never had the conversation opened deeper wounds.

Shuffling, trundling, blundering, the dancers frequently threatened to tumble over the balusters. Miss Hare held her heart, and Mrs Jolley her breath. In spite of the fascination of the arabesques it was possible to spin out of air and music, at the risk of death, the mistress preferred to see the one-step. It was so much kinder to the long beauties, working so hard and sad, as they pushed against the tum-ti-tum.

It was terribly sad, in the great, tatty, brilliant rooms, in mirror and memory.

Miss Hare really had to protest at last.

"Stop! Please, stop!" she called, and the strings which controlled her actions mercifully held up her hand.

Then the dancers stopped. Mrs Jolley stopped.

"Thank you," gasped Miss Hare. "I cannot be expected to experience too much in one day."

She was almost extinguished beneath the snuffer of her heavy hat.

Mrs Jolley was surprised, and might have sounded more reprov-
ing if breathlessness had not prevented it.

"You have led me such a dance," she said. "You could have
broken both our necks, but I hardly like to offer criticism, not in my
position, and because we know there are times when you are not in
full possession of yourself. Even so."

"Full possession?" asked Miss Hare.

So softly.

The housekeeper wondered whether she had gone too far, then
decided to go farther. It was her opportunity.

"You will not remember an evening on the terrace"—Mrs Jolley
was in a hurry—"or what you said, or what you did, or how you
passed out cold."

"Which evening on the terrace?" asked Miss Hare.

Softly.

"I cannot be expected to trot out dates." Mrs Jolley's teeth
snapped. "Or quote exact words. But I had the marks on my wrists
for several days."

"I *hurt* you?"

"I'll say! And might have done real damage if you hadn't passed
right out."

"And I can remember *nothing*."

"It was like a kind of fit."

An undulating dread threatened to drown Miss Hare.

"I told you nothing?" she had to ask. "Nothing of importance?"

"That depends on what is important."

"Tell me," Miss Hare ordered.

Mrs Jolley wondered whether she would.

"Tell me, Mrs Jolley," the mistress was insisting.

Then Mrs Jolley changed her tactics, partly because she sensed
an impending *coup de grâce,* partly since she was a little bit afraid.

"It was about the Chariot."

She inserted the remark, nor would fear prevent her watching the
result.

"I will not be told lies!" Miss Hare shouted.

"The truth is always truest when other people call it lies," Mrs Jolley answered in her triumph.

"You are a wicked, evil woman!" Miss Hare accused. "I knew it! All along I knew it!"

"Who is not wicked and evil, waiting for chariots at sunset, as if they was taxis?"

"Oh, you are bad, bad!" Miss Hare confirmed.

"And you are sick. I was foolish not to have called a doctor, but did not, well, out of respect for feelings."

"You must never call a doctor. Never, never!"

"I will not be here," said Mrs Jolley, "long."

"You will be with your thoughts, and that will be worse."

"What do you know about my thoughts?"

"Only what you have told me."

Mrs Jolley had some difficulty in releasing the handfuls of her apron.

"If we are two of a kind," she mumbled.

Miss Hare could not accept the possibility of that, and was rootling in remote recesses for some evidence of her own election.

"What did I really say?" she coaxed. "That evening? On the terrace?"

But Mrs Jolley was sulking.

If Miss Hare had not felt so exhausted, she might have known more alarm. There was a hornet crying as it built its nest in a doorway. The housekeeper had evaporated in her usual manner. A windy desert, somewhere, could not have been emptier than the hornet's cry suggested.

Yet, it was one of the lusher mornings of spring, after the grass had taken over. The immediate world appeared to be living under grass. Light was no longer distributed by the sun in honest golden metal; it oozed, a greenish, steamy yellow, from the flesh of grass. As Miss Hare went out into the green prevalence, the arrowheads of grass pricked her; she was the target of thousands. But had experienced worse, of course. So she went on.

She went down, through the militant, sharp, clattering grass, and through patches of shade where the soft, indolent swathes lolled and stank. She went to where the orchard had once been, and which she had not visited, it seemed to her, for years. Neglect, however, had not cancelled celebration. The tangle of staggy trees paraded a fresh

varnish, stuck by intermittent grace with virgin heads of blossom.
There was the plum tree, too, the largest anyone had ever seen.

The plum had obviously reached the height of its glory for that
year. Its crowded white dared the grass, brought the colour back to
the sky. The sun had returned, moreover, in its own right, and hung
a spangled banner on the tree.

Miss Hare went on pushing through the musky grass. She could
have swum forever, on her wave, towards the island of her tree,
holding out her hands, no longer begging for rescue, but in recogni-
tion.

And he came out from under the branches, from where he had
been sitting, apparently.

"Oh," she said then, and stopped, knee-deep in the waves of
grass.

He stood outside the tree waiting for her, though it was nobody she
had ever seen.

"I came in here," said the man. "I saw the tree."

"Yes," she said. "It is mine. Isn't it lovely? And I have not noticed it for years."

She was making little grunting sounds, of happiness, and recogni-
tion.

The man appeared to recognize, or, at least, not to reject.

Which was comforting.

He was a very ugly man, and strange, she saw.

"Would you care to sit down, in the shade," she asked, "and enjoy
the tree?"

She was filled with such a contentment of warmth and light she
would not have cared if he had refused. She had been refused so
regularly.

But the man did not reject her offer.

"I am Himmelfarb," he said, correctly, but oddly.

"Oh, yes?" she answered.

At the same time they stooped to negotiate the branches, which
were to provide their canopy.

PART TWO

Chapter 5

W H E N they were seated, on two stones which could have
been put there for them at the roots of the tree, the two people
ignored each other for a moment, staring back at the material world
as if to take a last look at those familiar forms which further experience might soon remove from their lives. From inside their flowered
tent, they could now observe how the masses of the orchard were
broken by a hatching in grey wood. Only precariously alive, the trees
were the greener for their sickliness, moodily defiant of the strong
light, with little, wizened oranges radiating a feverish gold. All was
most extraordinarily exposed to mind and view from beneath the
plum, and could have appeared to challenge hope, if it had not been
for the evidence of continuity: a bird cupped in the grey goblet of
her nest, a litter of young rabbits moving by clockwork into grass,
the eyelids of a lizard denying petrifaction by the sun. It was perfectly still, except that the branches of the plum tree hummed with
life, increasing, and increasing, deafening, swallowing them up.

At that point Mary Hare turned to her companion, wondering whether he was the kind of person to whom apologies had to be
made.

"This," she said, "is what I am really interested in." She wished
her hands could have helped her out, but they would not. "All these
things, I mean,"—making an awkward motion with her head—"are
what I understand."

She realized she was at her most hopelessly inadequate. Her tongue
was small, and round, and hard.

The man nodded, however. She saw he would take her seriously.
So she eased her knees, in their ugly brown woollen stockings.

"It is still difficult for us to appreciate, except in theory," said the man. "Until so very recently, we were confined within ghettoes. Trees and flowers grew the other side of walls, the other side of our experience, in fact."

Miss Hare made rather a face for the difficulties she had begun already to encounter.

"I must tell you something," she said. "I did not receive much education. My father was impatient. And then," she confided—it was terribly hard, but necessary—"I was supposed to be simple. Still, there were always a great many things I was able to understand."

The man could not have been less surprised, or perhaps he was excessively grave.

"I mean," he continued, "I am a Jew, and centuries of history have accustomed one to look inward instead of outward."

"Oh," said Miss Hare, "there are others who do that!"

And paused.

"Sometimes it is quite horrible," she murmured.

A prickly stillness had fallen round them.

Then she reached forward and jerked off, clumsily but successfully, a twig from her tree.

"There," she said, showing him.

She was holding the blossom in her blunt grubs of fingers. Would he be disgusted by her as many people were?

He bent forward to look at the flower. She had never been so close to a man—even her father's moments of intimacy had been necessarily distant; he had always avoided any gesture that might have developed into an embrace—so, now it was natural that she should observe intently. She was looking into the little whorls of hair on his neck, just above the collar. The confusion and profusion of rather wiry, once-black hair excited her love for all living matter, while she felt as guilty as though she had discovered the secret a respected friend had not attempted to conceal.

The man was taking a somewhat exaggerated interest in the plum blossom.

"It is almost finished," he was saying.

"It is only beginning," she corrected. "After this there will be a period that a lot of people consider dull. Little pin-heads of green fruit. Before the fat, purple, powdered ones.

"But the worms come, too," she remembered. "The plums will be full of worms."

All the time she was examining the pores of his skin. His ugly face had not yet opened to her, although she could feel there was nothing such a person would willingly hide. His face was stone, but must have possessed the warmth of statues in summer, which retain the heat of the sun after it has withdrawn. She was particularly fascinated by his great nose. It should have been cruel, but, on the contrary, it appeared so gentle she would have liked to touch it.

"You investigate nature very thoroughly," the man said, and laughed.

"I do not have to investigate," she answered. "By now, I know!"

Then she blushed for what Peg might have called a boast.

He continued looking at the twig, although each knew the necessity had passed. Her hands took the blossom for granted, while continuing gently to hold, and he was reminded of some animals: dogs that have accepted the good faith of a master, cats resuming their suckling of a litter while a stranger looks on. In their freckled clumsiness, her hands appeared supremely trustful.

"I am afraid I did not catch your name," her voice had begun to say, in the accents of another, a mother, perhaps, or governess.

"Himmelfarb," he said.

"Oh, dear!" she protested. "That is something I shall never learn. Haven't you something easier?"

"Mordecai."

"Worse!" she cried. "Much worse!"

And looked helpless, but pleased.

"I have been called by a great variety of names. Many of them in the heat of the moment. But in the end, no name is necessary," he said. "Not even the rightful ones."

She looked down into her lap to avoid something she did not fully understand.

"Mine are very simple," she ventured, and was almost too ashamed to disclose them.

But, when finally she did, he appeared delighted, and asked with some enthusiasm, "Did you realize it is possible to distinguish the figure of a hare if one looks carefully at the moon?"

"No. I did not. But I am not at all surprised," she replied earnestly.

"The sacrificial animal."

"What is that?" she asked, or panted.

"In some parts of the world, they believe the hare offers itself for sacrifice."

"Oh, no!" she cried. "I do not like to believe that. One meets with too many knives by the way, without going deliberately in search of one."

"The concept of the willing hare is surely less painful than that of the scapegoat, dragged out, bleating, by its horns."

"Goats? Please, don't tell me! I really do not understand any of these things."

His natural and immediate silence calmed her, however, and she said, "I don't think I ever met a Jew. Perhaps one. An old man who was useful to my father. A piano tuner. Are Jews so very different?"

"There is all the difference in the world."

"Do you like it?"

"We have no alternative."

"I understand," she said. "I, too, am different."

He laughed, and picked up the twig of wilting plum blossom which she had let fall.

"That would appear, mathematically and morally, to make us equal," he said. "I am glad."

Without irony, though. So that she was glad in turn. This Jew would not be one to go laughing at her.

"In the factory where I work," the Jew told her, and he had returned inward, behind walls higher than those he had mentioned, "I am considered the most different of all human beings."

"Of course!" she cried. "*They* always behave like that. What do you make in your factory? Is it close? I cannot imagine it. Tell me," she said.

"It is at Barranugli. We do make other things, but our particular item is bicycle lamps."

"I should hate that!" she replied with great vehemence. "But do you live close? I do hope."

"At Sarsaparilla," he said.

"Yes?"

"Below the post-office."

"In your own house?"

"So to speak."

"Yes, yes. I do know a little brown house. Oh, a house is better! One can hide in a house."

Until seeming to remember. Then she added, "Up to a point."

This mad, botched creature might subject him to thumbscrews, and touch him with feathers, at one and the same time, the Jew suspected.

"I have a house," she continued warily. "Down there. Beyond the orchard. Perhaps I shall show you some day. We shall see."

Because the Jew must understand the essential mystery and glory which Mrs Jolley and her like could never recognize. Yes, glory, because decay, even the putrid human kind, did not necessarily mean an end.

"I am not very often free."

The man seemed uneasy. He was not refusing. Rather, he was attempting to resist something which he might have desired.

"I know," said Miss Hare. "The factory. But you must breathe sometimes. Even a plant must breathe."

Her own breath had begun to sound spasmodic, though triumphant. She had never spoken like this before to any human being. Unexpected seeds of thought were germinating in her mind, and she had the impression she might shortly grasp things which had remained, hitherto, the secrets of others.

"Several times I have trespassed in your orchard," the Jew confessed, "and sat beneath your tree."

"That is a beginning," the woman suggested gently.

As a child she had learnt to help fledglings onto twigs, and maimed or frightened animals to walk.

"So you will come here again, won't you?" Now she was pleading, only this time it could have been in her own interests. "I want you to tell me things. About your life. Won't you?"

She was quite greedy. Her hands were helping to trap those words which eluded her.

"There are a great many details, incidents, which you could not hope to understand," the Jew replied, colder, it sounded. "Naturally."

"Oh, yes," she agreed. "There is always so much one does not understand. But it does not matter. Because some little thing, something quite unimportant, will show. So clearly. One is almost blinded by it," she gasped.

Suddenly she was choking with ideas and words. She did hope he would not consider her an imbecile.

With the result that the Jew was ashamed of the momentary feeling of repulsion she had roused in him. Nor was his remorse unrelated to a sensation experienced on somewhat similar occasions, when, for usually superficial reasons, his own feelings caused him to reject inwardly a member of his race.

"It is a long and involved story," he confessed, sinking down against the trunk of the tree, so that the bark scored the back of his neck, without his being aware. "Perhaps I shall tell you some of it," he said. "Another time."

But the strange part of it was: he began, there and then, whether he realized or not, and perhaps he did not, until fully launched, in giving the woman the most intimate, sometimes the most horrible details of all that had ever happened to him. But, of course, in that sultry, motionless air, it was like addressing some animal, or not even that. He remembered seeing fungi which suggested existence of the most passive order. And she could become perfectly still. It was only later that he recoiled from such an attitude, as if he had been guilty of treading on life.

But now, beneath the tree, booming with bees and silence, he had gone right back, drowsily, painfully, exquisitely, into memory. He had hardly ever allowed himself before.

And the woman listened.

"Yes?" she would murmur, but only in the beginning; or: "Oh, dear, no! No, no, no!"

With her hands she would try to ease the air of some difficulty they were experiencing together, or wrestle with impending terrors.

Mordecai Himmelfarb was born in the North German town of Holunderthal, to a family of well-to-do merchants, some time during the eighteen-eighties. Moshe, the father, was a dealer in furs, through connections in Russia, many of whom crossed Germany while Mordecai was still a child. The reason for their move had been discussed, mostly behind closed doors, by uncles and aunts, accompanied by the little moans of distress with which his mother received any report of injustice to their race. If Moshe the father remained the wrong side of the door, preferring to stroke his son's head, or even to take a beer at the *Stübchen,* it was not from lack of sympathy, but because he was a sensitive man. Any such crisis disturbed him so severely, he preferred to believe it had not occurred.

Mordecai the child observed the stream of relatives which poured in suddenly, and away: the cousins from Moscow and Petersburg, no longer quite so rich or so glossy; their headachy, emotional wives, clinging to the remnants of panache, and still able to produce surprises, little objects in cloisonné and brilliants, out of the secret pocket in a muff. The whole of this colourful rout was sailing, they told him, for America, to liberty, justice, and the future. He watched them go, through the wrought-iron grille, from his own safe, German hall.

There were the humbler Russians, too: people in darker, dustier clothes, who had suffered the same indignities, whom his mother received with reverent affection, his father with an increase in his usual joviality. There was, in particular, the Galician rabbi, whose face Mordecai could never after visualize, but remembered, rather, as a presence and a touch of hands.

Pogroms had reduced this distant cousin of his mother's to the clothes he wore and the faith he lived. Whatever his destination, he had paused for a moment at the house on the Holzgraben in Holunderthal, where his cousin had taken him into the small, rather dark room which she used for calls of a private nature, and the visits of embarrassed relatives. The mother sat, dressed as always by then, in black, smoothing her child's hair. But without looking at him, the little boy saw. In the obscure room, talking to the foreign rabbi, for the greater part in a language the boy himself had still to get, his mother had grown quite luminous. He would have liked to continue watching the lamp that had been lit in her, but from some impulse of delicacy decided, instead, to lower his eyes. And then he had become, he realized, the object of attention. His mother was drawing him forward, towards the centre of the geometric carpet. And the rabbi was touching him. The rabbi, of almost womanly hands, was searching his forehead for some sign. He was laying his hands on the diffident child's damp hair. Talking all the time with his cousin in the foreign tongue. While the boy, inwardly resisting less, was bathed in the stream of words, suspended in a cloud of awe.

Finally, his father had come in, more than ever jovial, shooting his shiny cuffs, and arranging his already immaculate moustache, with its distinct hairs and lovely, lingering scent of pomade. Laughing, of course—because Moshe did laugh a lot, sometimes spontaneously, sometimes also when at a loss—he joined his wife and her cousin in their conversation, though he altered the complexion of it.

And said at last, in German, not exactly his own, "Well, Mordecai, quite the little zaddik!"

And continued laughing, not out of malice—he was too agreeable for that. If his wife forgave him his lapse in taste, it was because he had often been proved a good man at heart.

Moshe Himmelfarb was a worldly Jew of liberal tastes. Success led him by a manicured hand, and continued to dress him with discretion. Nothing excessive about Moshe, unless it was his phiz, which would suddenly jar on those tolerant souls who collected Jews, and make them wonder at their own eccentricity. Not that relations were thereby impaired. Moshe, in deep appreciation of the liberation, and truly genuine affection for the *goyim,* would not allow that. And he was right, of course. All those emancipated Jews of his acquaintance were ready to support him in his claim that the age of enlightenment and universal brotherhood had dawned at last in Western Europe. Jews and *goyim* were taking one another—intermittently, at least —moist-eyed to their breasts. The old, dark days were done. Certainly there remained the problem of Eastern Europe, and deplorable incidents often occurred. Everybody knew that, and had been personally affected, but the whole house could not be swept clean at once. In the meantime, money was raised by Western Jewry to assist the victims, and to all such funds Moshe was always the first to subscribe. He loved to give, whether noticeably generous sums to numerous religious missions, the works of the German poets to his son, or presents of wine and cigars to those gentiles who allowed themselves to be cultivated, and with whom he was so deeply, so gratefully in love.

Happy are the men who are able to tread transitional paths, scarcely looking to left or to right, and without distinguishing an end. Moshe Himmelfarb was one of them. If he had seldom been the object of direct criticism, except in trivial, family matters, it was because he had always taken care not to offer himself as a target. Unlike certain fanatics, he recognized his obligations to the community in which he lived, while observing the ceremony of his own. Mordecai remembered the silk hats in which his father presented himself, on civic and religious occasions alike. Ordered from an English hatter, Moshe's hats reflected that nice perfection which may be attained by the reasonable man. For Moshe Himmelfarb was nothing less. If he was also nothing more, that was after other, exacting, not to say reactionary standards, by which such lustrous hats could only be judged vain, hollow, and lamentably fragile.

Yet, along with his shortcomings, and his acquaintances, many of them men of similar mould, smelling of prosperity and cigars, and filled with every decent intention, Moshe continued to attend the synagogue in the Schillerstrasse. That they did not grow haggard, like some, from obeying the dictates of religion, was because they were reasonable, respectful, rather than religious men, and might have pointed out, if they had been openly accused, and if they had dared, that the Jewish soul was at last set free. The walls were down, the suffocating rooms were burst open, the chains of observance had been loosed.

They would still sway, however, all those worldly Jews of the synagogue in the Schillerstrasse, when the wind of prayer smote them. Standing beside his father, the little boy would watch, and wait to be carried in the same direction. He would stroke the fringes of his father's tallith, or bury his face in the soft folds. He would wait for his father to beat his breast for all the sins that were shut up inside. Then he himself would overflow with a melancholy joy that all was right in the forest of Jews in which he stood. All the necks were so softly swathed in wool, that, however fat and purple some of them looked, he was comforted, and would glance up, towards the gallery directly opposite, where he knew his mother to be. But behind the lattice. The boy would not see her, except in his mind's eye, where she sat very still and clear.

For Mordecai the man, his mother remained a sculptured figure. Whether, in fact, life and fashion had influenced her sufficiently to create a continuously evolving series of identities, his memory presented her as a single image: black dress; the high collar of net and whalebone, relieved by a little, seemly frill; the broad, yellowish forehead, marked with the scars of compassionate thought; eyes in which the deceits of this world were regretfully, but gently drowned; the mouth that overcame secret ailments, religious doubts, and all but one bitterness.

It was evident from the beginning that the boy was closer to the mother, although it was only much later established that she had given him her character. To casual acquaintances it was surprising that the father, so agreeable, so kind, so generous, did not have a greater influence. By contrast the mother made rather a sombre impression, stiff, and given to surrounding herself with certain dark, uncouth, fanatically orthodox Jews, usually her relatives. Of course, the boy loved and honoured his good father, and would laugh and chatter with him as required, or listen gravely as the beauties of Goethe or the other poets were pointed out. So that Moshe was delighted with his son, and would bring expensive presents: a watch, or a brass telescope, or collected works bound in leather. But it was out of the mother's silence and solitude of soul that the rather studious, though normal, laughing, sometimes too high-spirited little boy had been created.

Frau Himmelfarb had never become reconciled to the well-ordered, too specious life of the North German town. As she walked with her child against the painted drop of Renaissance houses, or formal magnificence of Biedermeier mansions, her incredulous eyes would reject the evidence that men had thus confined the infinite. Only in certain dark mediaeval streets, Mordecai remembered, did his mother seem to escape from the oppression of her material surroundings. She herself would blur, as strange, apparently inexpressible words came struggling softly out of her mouth, and her feet would almost dance as she hurried over the uneven cobbles, skipping the puddles of dirty water, very light. She would visit numbers of the rather smelly, frightening houses, and bring presents, and examine children, whether for ailments, or their knowledge of God, and even hitch up her skirt over her petticoat, before going down on her knees to scrub a floor neglected by the sick. Along the airless alleys, in the dark houses of the Jewish poor, his mother's Galician spirit was released—which, in his memory, had seldom happened anywhere else, unless during the visit of her cousin, the destitute rabbi, in their own anteroom, or while writing letters to her many other relatives.

The mother was one of a scattered family. It was her sorrow, and pride. She liked to bring her writing things, as though she had been a visitor, and sit at the round table, with its cloth of crimson plush, in preference to the ormolu desk on which Moshe had lovingly insisted. Then the little boy would play with the plush pompons, and occasionally glance at the letters as they grew, and shuffle the used envelopes, from which she would allow him later to soak the stamps.

He had known his mother, on a single rainy afternoon, seal envelopes for Poland, Rumania, the United States, even China and Ecuador. Until, finally, there was nothing of her left to give.

He realized only very much later the important part her dispersed family had played in his mother's secret life: how, in her mind, their omnipresence might have ensured and hastened redemption for the whole world. Such a conviction, implied, though certainly never expressed, gave her a kind of distinction amongst the numerous pious ladies who were always in transit through her house, eating *Streuselkuchen* and drinking coffee, organizing charitable projects, announcing births, marriages, and deaths, daring sometimes even to indulge, in the presence of their hostess, in bursts of frivolous, not to say unseemly chat. But always returning to one point. The women clung together like a ball of brown bees, driven by the instinct of their faith, intoxicated with the honey of their God.

The presence of that God amongst the walnut furniture of the sumptuous house—for Himmelfarbs had moved from above the shop before Mordecai was able to remember—was unquestioned by the worldly, but prudently respectful Moshe, taken for granted by the little boy, even by the confident young man who the latter eventually became, and who turned sceptical not of his religion, rather, of his own need for it. Religion, like a winter overcoat, grew oppressive and superfluous as spring developed into summer, and the natural sources of warmth were gradually revealed. But there was no mistaking the love and respect the young man kept for the enduring qualities of his old, discarded coat. In the solstice of his self-love, in the heat of physical ardour, he would melt with nostalgia at the thought of it.

In the meantime, however, the little boy remained wrapped in the warm reality of the garment they had given him to wear.

When he was only six, the mother remarked with the casualness she always adopted for important matters, "Do you realize, Moshe, it is time the child began to receive instruction?"

"Yoy!" The father, who loved his own joke, winced to express horror. "Do you want to load the boy already? And worst of all, with Hebrew?"

"Yes," she answered, seriously. "It is our own tongue."

Moshe was often inclined to wonder how he had come to marry his wife. Whom he loved, however. So it was agreed.

It was usual for the boys of their acquaintance to attend the classes of Herr Ephraim Glück, the melamed, but because of some special confidence the mother had, the Cantor Katzmann was engaged to teach her son the alphabet. Which the latter mastered at astonishing speed. And began shortly to write phrases, and recite prayers. And grew vain. He would turn his head aside, and mumble what he already knew too well, or declaim too loudly, with a shameful spiritual arrogance.

On one occasion the Cantor was forced to mention, "If a Jew is proud, Mordecai, it is all the harder when he bites the dust. As he certainly will."

The Cantor himself was a humble man, with several squint-eyed children, and a wife who nagged. His voice was his only glory. When it had been poured out to the dregs, he would appear emptied indeed, falling back upon his chair with a smile of deathly content. Mordecai remembered him especially after the climax of Rosh Hashanah, and Yom Kippur, when, it could have been, the Cantor had attempted the impossible. The white closed eyelids would not so much as flutter, as he sat and smiled faintly from behind them. He was a small man, and his pupil loved him in memory, more than he had respected him in life.

At the age of ten, the boy entered the Gymnasium. Already before *bar mitzvah,* he had embarked on Greek, Latin, French, with English for preference. He had begun to carry off the prizes. Sources, both informed and uninformed, insisted that Mordecai ben Moshe was exceptionally brilliant.

"You see, Malke," the father remarked, preparing in his mind an additional, expensive prize, "our Martin is surely intended to become a man of some importance."

Because he had developed the ridiculous and distasteful habit of calling their son by a German name, his wife would pinch her eyebrows together as if suffering physical pain, although she would let it be known that, in spite of her expression of torture, she was grateful for the boy's success.

"*Ach,*" she exclaimed. "Yes," she said, and found she had a cough. "We have known from the beginning he was no fool."

How her cough continued to rack her.

"But," she was able at last to resume, "all that is by the way. I only ask that Mordecai shall be remembered as a man of faith."

So that the father's pleasure was cut by his wife's stern consistency, and in time he ceased to love, while continuing to honour. In his casual, but always amiable way, he allowed her to bear many of the burdens, because he saw she was suited to it, and she succeeded manfully, for, inside her rather delicate body, she had considerable strength of mind.

Alone with her son, she would often unbend, even after he was grown. She would become quite skittish in her private joy, with the result that the boy was sometimes ashamed for what appeared unnecessary, not to say unnatural, in one of natural dignity.

"Mordecai ben Moshe!" she would refer to him half aloud, half laughing.

To establish, as it were, an unmistakable identity.

She had the habit of forming in his presence a suggestion of ideas, sometimes in German, more often in Yiddish, and as he learnt to follow her murmur, he forged a chain out of it. There were many tales, too, of relatives and saints. She could become inspired. Her Seder table was the materialization of simple dogma. For the rites of the Sabbath she had a particular genius, and, watching the candles increase in light and stature as her hands coaxed, her husband was again convinced of his own genuine desire to worship.

By far the most agreeable of all the feast days observed by the family on the Holzgraben was that of Succoth, for it made the least spiritual demands on the father, or so the son began to sense. Ignoring, for some atavistic reason, the considerable triangular garden, with its smell of toadstools and damp leaves, they improvised their tabernacle beneath the lattice on the balcony. The meals could not appear too often or too soon, which they ate beneath the stars at Succoth, above the *Stadtwald* at Holunderthal. The symbols of citron and palm flourished happily in the father's somewhat shallow mind. Because, by now it had been made clear, the bleak heights of Atonement were not for Moshe, only the foothills of Thanksgiving. In the circumstances, the additional duty laid upon the mother was a source of embarrassment to the parents, also in time, the father suspected, to the son. On returning home from the synagogue, after the travail and exhaustion of Yom Kippur, he might pinch the boy's cheek, and look into his eyes, and wonder to which side Mordecai was going to be drawn. As his hopes conflicted with his fears, Moshe would sigh, and again, more loudly, when the first mouthful of reviving coffee passed his lips.

The hopes of all converged upon *bar mitzvah*. The candidate approached the ceremony with a dangerous amount of confidence. He received the phylacteries and the shawl, together with many desirable presents from parents, uncles, aunts, and cousins. He delivered ringingly, and with a sculptural logic, his discourse on the chosen subject, with the result that aunts turned to congratulate one another long before he had finished. They could have devoured the feverish face—to some extent a replica of each of theirs—underneath the plastered hair and pretty *Käppchen*. Mordecai was entranced, and did not listen continuously to anybody's voice, unless it was his own. Somewhere behind him on the platform wandered the father who was relinquishing, not without a hint of tears, spiritual responsibility. There were some amongst Frau Himmelfarb's relatives who could not contain their ironic smiles on noticing poor Malke's Moshe. But were immediately recalled to a state of adequate reverence by a flash of silver from the Scrolls. After the ceremony, there was a delicious meal, at which the formally dedicated boy was caressed and flattered. His triumph made him proud, shy, exalted, indifferent, explosively hilarious, and uncommunicative of his true feelings—if he was conscious of what they were.

Who, indeed, could tell which way the *bar mitzvah* boy would go? Certainly not the self-congratulating father, perhaps the mother, through the tips of her fingers, or subtler colloquy of souls.

In the comfortable, but ugly house, in the closed circle of relatives and friends, protected by the wings of angels, illuminated by the love of God, Mordecai accepted the pattern which his race, his religion, and his parents had ordained. But there was, in addition, an outside world, which his mother feared, for which his father yearned, and of which Mordecai became increasingly aware. There the little waxen, silent boy grew into a bony, rasping youth, the dark down straggling like an indecision on his upper lip, the lips themselves blooming far too soon, the great nose assuming manifest importance. It was the age of mirrors, and in their surfaces Mordecai attempted regularly to solve the mystery of himself. He was growing muscular, sensual, yellow: hideous to some, provocative to others. What else, nobody was yet allowed to see.

"Tell me, you ugly Jew, what it feels like to be one?" his friend Jürgen Stauffer asked.

In fun, of course. Friendship and laughter still prevailed. The forest flecked the boys' skins, as they rubbed along, elbow to elbow, the soles of their boots made slippery by thicknesses of fallen leaves.

"Tell me!" Jürgen laughed, and insisted.

He was of that distinctive tint of German gold, affection showing in the shallows of his mackerel eyes.

"Oh, like something that runs on a hundred legs," Himmelfarb replied. "Or no legs at all. A snake, for instance. Or scorpion. Anyway, specially created to be the death of gentiles."

Then they laughed louder, and together. Sundays had become warmer than the Sabbath for the young Jew, when he walked with his friend, Jürgen Stauffer, on the wilder side of the *Stadtwald* at Holunderthal.

"Tell me," Jürgen asked, "about the Passover sacrifice."

"When we kill the Christian child?"

"So it seems!"

How Jürgen laughed.

"And cut him up, and drink the blood, and put slices in a *Brötchen* to send the parents?" Mordecai had learnt how to play.

"*Ach, Gott!*" Jürgen Stauffer laughed.

How his teeth glistened.

"Old Himmelfurz!" he cried. "*Du liebes Rindvieh!*"

Then they were hitting each other, and grunting. Their skins were melting together. They could not wrestle enough on the beds of leaves. Afterwards they lay panting, and looked up through the exhausted green, to discuss a future still incalculable, except for the sustaining thread of friendship. In the silences they would sigh beneath the weight of their affection for each other.

"But when I become a cavalry officer—and there is no question of anything else, because of Uncle Max—and you are the professor of languages, it is not very likely we shall ever see each other again," Jürgen Stauffer reasoned.

"Then you must arrange to ride your horses," Mordecai suggested, "round and round whichever university I honour with my presence."

"It is a vice, Martin, never to be serious. A hopeless, hopeless, vicious vice!"

From where he lay, Jürgen Stauffer thumped his friend.

"You are the hopeless one, not to choose a more civilized career."

"But I like horses," Jürgen protested. "And then I am also a bit stupid."

Himmelfarb could have kissed his friend.

"Stupid? You are the original ass!"

If they had not tired themselves out, they might have wrestled some more, but instead they lay and listened to the blaze of summer and their own contentment.

Occasionally the young Jew was invited to his friend's house, for the parents' liberal attitude allowed them to receive regardless of race. Gerhard Stauffer, the father, was, of course, the publisher. He even loved books, and an undeserved failure would make him suffer more than an obvious success would cause him to rejoice. His wife, a minor actress in her youth, had retired into life and marriage equipped with a technique for theatre. Frau Stauffer was able to convince a guest that the scene they had just enacted together contributed immensely to the play's success.

"Martin shall sit beside *me*," Frau Stauffer would emphasize, patting the place on the sofa with the touch the situation required. "Now that we are *comfortable*," she would decide, while inclining just that little in the direction of her guest, "you must tell me what you have been *doing*. Provided it has been *dis-reputable*. I refuse to listen to anything else. On such a *damp* afternoon, you must *curdle* my blood with indiscretions."

Then Frau Stauffer smiled that deliberate smile. She had remained of the opinion that any line may be "improved," and that every scene needed "lifting up."

But the boy was conscious of his lack of talent. Seated beside his hostess on her cloud, he remained the victim of his awkward body.

Or, advancing from an opposite direction, the host would court their unimportant guest, inviting him to give his point of view, showering newspaper articles and books.

"Have you discovered Dehmel?" Herr Stauffer might inquire, or: "What do you think, Martin, of Wedekind? I would be most interested to hear your honest opinion."

As if it mattered to that grave man.

The embarrassed boy was gratified, but could not escape too soon,

back to his friend. The attention of the parents flattered more in
retrospect.

"You see," said Jürgen, without envy, "you are the respected intellectual. I am the German stable-boy."

But it could have been for some such reason that the young Jew
admired his friend.

There was the elder brother, too, who would emerge mysteriously
from his room, suffering from acne and a slight astigmatism, and eating a slice of buttered bread. Konrad has outgrown his strength,
and must fortify himself, Frau Stauffer explained. Konrad came and
went, ignoring whatever existed outside the orbit of his own ego.
He seemed to despise in particular all younger boys—or was it only
the Jewish ones?—that was not yet made clear.

"What does he do all the time in his room?" Mordecai asked the
younger brother.

"He is studying," replied the latter, with the air of one who could
not be expected to take further interest. "He is all right," he said.
"Only a bit stuck-up."

On that occasion Konrad Stauffer came out of his room chewing at
a *Brötchen* with caraway seeds on top.

"What," he said to Mordecai, "you here again! Are you perhaps
en pension?"

As everybody else was embarrassed, he laughed a little for his
own joke.

There was the sister, Mausi, still a little girl. Her plaits glistened
like the tails of certain animals. Once she threw her arms round the
Jew's waist, and pressed against him with all her strength, and tried
to throw him.

"I am stronger than you!" she claimed.

But neither proved, nor provoked.

She stood laughing into the bosom of his shirt. Her breath burned
where the V opened on his bare skin.

Best and most alarming of all were evenings in the big salon,
when girls came in bows and sashes, their necks smelling of
kölnisches Wasser. There were girls already corseted stiff, and a few
real young men, often the sons of cavalry officers. These absolute
phenomena, themselves cadets, always knew what to do, with the
result that younger boys would listen humiliated to their own crude,

breaking voices, and mirrors reminded them that the pimples were still lurking in their tufts of down.

One evening, after their elders had withdrawn to the library to amuse themselves at cards, somebody of real daring devised the most scandalous game.

"Which person in the room do you like best?" it was asked of each in turn. "Why?" The next impossible question followed, and others, all headed in the inevitable, and most personal direction.

Giggles, and the braying of the adolescent jackass, widened the circles of embarrassment.

"Whom do you like, Mausi Stauffer?" finally it had to be asked.

Mausi Stauffer did not hesitate.

"Martin Himmelfarb," she said.

Some of the young ladies might have burst, if their whalebone had not contained them. In the circumstances, they rocked and wheezed.

"Why, Mausi?" asked Cousin Fritz, the son of Uncle Max.

The scar across his left cheek appeared unnaturally distinct.

"Because," said Mausi. "Because he is interesting, I suppose."

"Come, now!" complained an upright young woman in steel spectacles, with a pale, flat rosette of a mouth. "That is a weak answer. You may have to pay a forfeit. Fifty strokes on the palm of your hand from the edge of a ruler."

Mausi screamed. She could not have borne it.

"We want to give you another chance," said Cousin Fritz, so beautiful and hateful in his cadet's uniform. "*Why* does this Himmelfarb appeal to you?"

He made the name sound particularly exotic and ridiculous.

Mausi screamed. She tossed her plaits into the air.

"Because," she cried, and snickered, and wound her thin legs together, and perspired in her crushed muslin. "Because," she screeched, in a voice they were dragging out of her, "he is like"— she still hesitated—"a kind of black *buck!*"

The bronzes might have tumbled from their pedestals, if, at that moment, a spinster lady devoted to the family had not returned in search of her scarf, and decided instinctively to remain.

In that same moment, Mordecai made down the passage for the lavatory.

As he came out again, Konrad Stauffer was trying the door.

"Oh!" exclaimed Konrad, mostly with his stomach, and recoiled.

He looked quite pale, and blank, but could have been rehearsing a speech.

"Just a lot of stupid Germans," he managed to utter breathily. "Germans are all animals."

"Aren't we also Germans?" Mordecai suggested.

"Those who pass judgment always exclude themselves," the spotty young man replied, and laughed. "Haven't you found that out? Oh, dear!" He sighed. "I don't propose to get involved in anything else tonight. I am going up to my room."

Mordecai did not know what to make of Konrad.

Nor did he see him again for years. One result of the evening was that Frau Stauffer apparently decided to bring down the curtain on the comedy they had been enacting in their relationship with the young Jew. Jürgen grew increasingly elusive. Attempts at even indirect inquiry would start him kicking holes in the ground, or else he would mumble, and fix his eyes on some point which, he let it be understood, lay outside his friend's field of vision.

Often in this suffocating situation, Mordecai would struggle for breath. Then his mother, noticing his dark eyelids, and the colour of his skin, prescribed a tonic, and after only half a bottle he slept with a whore called Marianne, who lived beneath a gable in one of the older streets of the town. His body was flooded with a new, though at first dreadful, relief.

"You Jews!" Marianne remarked, looking him over during a pause, for which she was sufficiently generous not to charge. "The little bit they snip off only seems to make you hotter."

As for her client, he stared exhausted at her enormous beige nipples, and wondered whether his instincts would know how to navigate the frail craft in which he had embarked alone.

Thus committed to the flesh, the ceremonies of his parents' house soon became intolerable. The Sabbath, for instance, all through his boyhood a trance of innocent perfection, in which he would not have been surprised to see the Bride herself cross the threshold, was now transformed into a wilderness of hours, where good aunts and all those ugly girl cousins were continually setting traps of questions to catch his guilt. Prayers and food choked him equally as he waited for sunset and the scent of spices to wake him from his nightmare. Lovingly. And he, in turn, loved all that he was rejecting, not so much by choice, it seemed to him at first in moments of self-exon-

eration, but by arrangement between unknown persons who controlled his future.

The severest torture remained the trial by charity. There were
the humble, sometimes even ragged, unwashed individuals, whom
his father, from sense of duty, or the need for self-congratulation,
collected at the synagogue, and brought home to the Sabbath table,
where Martin-Mordecai would exert himself to offer friendly words.
and recommend the most delicious dishes, to atone for the disgust the
visitors roused in him. There was one creature in particular: a little
dyer, whose skin was bathed in indigo; the palms of his hands were
mapped indelibly in purple. This man's material affliction impressed
itself on his conscience the evening the dyer slipped while crossing
one of Moshe's handsome rugs. The boy felt himself to be in a way
responsible. As his hands slithered on the old Jew's greasy coat, he
grabbed hold of what seemed a handful of rag, and just prevented
the guest from falling. But his own fright and nausea were
in his mouth; he might have been the one who had all but suffered
a serious fall, whereas the old man grew servile with gratitude for
what he called a gentlemanly act, was moved to caress every inch of
his saviour's back, and to bestow pretentious titles such as Crutch
of the Infirm, and Protector of the Poor.

After Mordecai had escaped from the room, and was washing himself, his mother came and stood in the doorway, to say in her driest
voice, which tender feelings would force her to adopt, "You are upset, my dear boy, and have not yet experienced the hundredth part."

She watched her son thoughtfully.

"Dry your hands quickly now," she coaxed, gentler, "and come
on back to us. We must not allow that poor man to guess."

She would have liked to use her compassion to comfort those near-
est to her, but the loving woman was unable to. More often than not,
she saw her words salt the wounds.

The house was full of twilight situations, and shaken attitudes.
The son became amused. He would raise one shoulder and compose
his mouth, as the Kiddush introduced the Sabbath. He would barb
the words of prayers with mockery, to aim at innocent targets.
Even though he failed to destroy what he had loved most, his per-
versity had developed to the point where the attempt remained his
painful substitute for ritual.

Then, as soon as his duties had been at least outwardly discharged, he would rush out. He would roam the streets, looking into lit windows, brush against passers-by, and apologize with an effusiveness which could only be interpreted as insolence. Now that he was filled with a rage to live, the scents of the streets maddened him. He would try the breasts of the whores, propped on cushions, on their window-sills. He had an insatiable appetite for white flesh, of pale complaisant German girls, pressed against stucco, or writhing in the undergrowth of parks, beside stagnant water, in a smell of green decay.

If he had not hardened quickly, he might have been consumed by his own disgust.

But he grew steely. He plastered down his wingèd hair. He wore a moustache. And studied.

All through the period of his worst disintegration, Mordecai remained, to the innocent and unaware, dedicated solely to his books. He did, in fact, cling to them, like fingers to a raft. And what more solid and reasonable than words as such? It was only in the permutations and combinations that they dissolved into that same current which threatened to suck down the whole boiling, grinning crew of desperate, drowning souls.

At the university the young man's intellectual activities were narrowed down to the study of his preferred language—English. Its bland and rather bread-like texture became his manna. But, in opposition to his will and intentions, he would find his mind hankering after the obdurate tongue he had got as a boy from the Cantor Katzmann. His proficiency in Hebrew had grown with intermittent attention, and he would often read, late at night, both for instruction, and for the bitter pleasure of it.

In the second decade of the century Mordecai Himmelfarb received his doctorate in English, and shortly after, was informed that he would be permitted to continue his studies at the University of Oxford.

Moshe was overjoyed, not only for the impression the event would make on his acquaintances, but because of his admiration for the English, for the excellent quality of their cloth, boots, and the silk hats he liked to wear on formal occasions. If he also sensed the distance which separated the English temperamentally from himself, that added, if anything, to their fascination. And now his own son was to be removed to the side of the elect. The gap in their relationship, already wide, would necessarily widen. Already the old man visualized himself, the self-sacrificing Jewish father, standing on railway platforms in the steam from trains. The joyous, painful tears spurted in anticipation. For that which moved and charmed Moshe most, was that which receded irretrievably: departing trains, the faces of the *goyim,* the relationship with his own son, and, if he had dared to think, let alone whisper—he who contributed so generously to the Zionist movement—the redemption of Israel as a possible event.

It was Moshe who broke the news to the boy's mother, and in that way, perhaps, less pain was caused.

Frau Himmelfarb, who was darning a sock, did not at first answer. She continued looking at the sock with the rather myopic patience characteristic of her.

"I did expect, Malke, that you would grasp," her husband had begun to emphasize, "the immense advantage it will give the boy if he decides on an academic career."

His wife was looking closely at the sock.

"Well?" he asked, and reasonably, but was immediately driven to support his argument, not exactly by ranting, but almost: "It is time we Jews recognized the world has changed!" Here Moshe actually trembled. "All the opportunities that are open to us now!"

"Ah, Moshe! Moshe!" sighed the woman, in the way that had always irritated him most.

"That is not an answer!" he protested.

"However you and others may transform him," his wife replied, "I pray that God will recognize a good Jew."

"It is of more importance today," said the father, "that the world should recognize a good man."

All of which was heard, as it happened, by their son, who had come in, and was listening with that cynical, yet affectionate amusement with which he now received any idea that originated in his parents.

"Ah, Moshe"—his mother sighed again—"you forget that when both kinds are divided up into good, bad, and indifferent, the Jews will remain distinct from men."

"There you are!" fumed the father, realizing at last that his son was present. "I make the simple announcement that you will be going to Oxford, and your mother embarks on a philosophical, not to say racial argument. Of Jews and men! I hope I am a man! What are you?"

"I would like to think I am both," the young fellow replied, "but sometimes wonder whether I am anything at all."

Because this was nothing like what he had intended to say, Mordecai smiled.

"Then it has come to that!" cried the mother. "There, Moshe! Where can it all end?"

In her distress she kept on turning and stretching the meticulously darned sock.

"That does not mean you may expect me to cut my throat!" the son continued, laughing, jerking up his chin, and baring his teeth in what had, this time, only the rudiments of a smile.

"It is terrible to see one's best intentions completely misinterpreted!" The father felt himself justified in moaning.

"Oh, but I do appreciate them!" the son answered with dutiful alacrity. "All you have ever done. All the kindnesses. You have been a good father. And you need not doubt I shall try to repay you."

Moshe Himmelfarb began to cry.

"And Mother," the son almost shouted, because of his father's emotion, and because the mere mention of his mother involved him more deeply than ever in the metaphysical thicket from which he was hoping to tear himself free. "Whose guidance," he babbled, his voice carrying him to a crescendo of melodrama of which he himself was most aware, "whose example and deeds, might well redeem the whole race. Excepting one who is beyond redemption!"

"We must certainly pray for you," Malke Himmelfarb remarked gently, hanging her head above the now crumpled and rejected sock. "My poor son!"

Long after he had rushed from the room, Mordecai continued to visualize the situation: the black hairs on his father's elegant, but frail and ineffectual wrist; the pulse, actual or imagined, in his mother's yellow temple; and the ornate, heartrending furniture, of which he had explored every grain, every crack and blemish, under cover of conversation, daydream, and prayer.

Now he would have prayed, but could not. He was suffering, and indeed continued to suffer from a kind of spiritual amnesia. Remembering an incident in the examination room, in which, at the end of an agonizing hour, the Italian language had flooded back into his mind, he hoped that some such release would take place on the present occasion—or he could have waited, weeks, if necessary, or even months.

But it did not.

At most, an occasional onset of compassion would deflect the blade of his cynicism, as on the evening when he watched his own father leave a fairground on the outskirts of the town, accompanied by a brewer's clerk named Goltz, known to him by sight and repute, and two anonymous girls of unmistakable occupation. As the young man watched from the shelter of a clump of pollarded trees, the bluish-white glimmer from the flares sluiced the faces of the three unsteady gentiles and their Jewish clown. The action of the flickering light made the unnatural abandon of the elderly, respectable Jew appear quite maniacal. He, too, was flickering and fluctuating as he led the way through the hubbub of shouting and jerky music. His companions seemed to have reached the stage where only the conventions of revelry are obeyed. The clerk stopped for a moment, and stuck his head inside a bush, to vomit. The mouths of the others opened from habit in the dreadful dough of their faces to emit song or wind. Or an arm attempted to return the imagined pressure of an arm. Or lips sucked the air in imitation of a kiss. So the revellers advanced, and almost brushed against their judge in passing. Without moving, the latter continued to watch, and was able to distinguish the pores of their skins, the roots of their hair, the specks of gold flashing in their teeth. If he did not catch their words, it was because those were drowned in the tumult of his distress, which continued long after the ridiculous old satyr, who was also his father, had disappeared. That his own desires were similar, that he had breathed on similar smeary faces, of similar sweaty girls, and fumbled at the scenty dresses, made the incident too familiar, and more intolerable.

Yet, the young man had lived long enough, if only by one day, to embrace his father on retiring the following night. For a moment he had stood behind the chair. There was the scraggy, reprehensible neck. Would he plunge his knife, which he had learnt to use with the skill of any shohet? Then the thought began to tremble in him: that reason is far too imperfect a weapon. So he had bent forward instead, and Moshe interpreted what he received as an expression of gratitude, not of pity. The old Jew was at once brimming over with pride, for the grateful son who appreciated all that was being done for him.

Very soon after, Mordecai left for Oxford. Although in those days the talk was of war, the Kaiser's unpredictable temper, and the refusal of the French nation to respect German ideals, it seemed most unlikely to the young man that an international situation would ignore the crucial stage in his career. Dressed in a topcoat of excellent, sober cloth and cut, and a travelling cap in tartan tweed, the kind thought of one of his aunts, he presented a fine figure as they stamped about the railway platform. They were all there. Moshe had fallen in love with the new leather monogrammed luggage, with which he had provided his son. But the mother could have been dazed by the appearances of a material world, of which she had only been allowed glimpses hitherto, and her clothes, as always on occasions of importance and splendour, looked as though they had been brought down from an attic. As for the son, he was only too relieved at the thought of relinquishing the identity with which his parents were convinced they had endowed him. And at last the train did pull out. And later in the day, the boat sailed into the fog.

At Oxford Himmelfarb continued to distinguish himself scholastically. Determined at the beginning to restrict himself to books, he soon discovered he was an influence on the lives of human beings. He was very prepossessing in his Semitic way. He developed an ease of manner. Men hoped for his respect, women competed for his heart, and he would always allow them to believe they had succeeded.

There was perhaps one young woman who roused and sustained his passionate interest. The young people went so far as to discuss marriage during their attachment, though neither thought to ask a parent's advice on the desirability of the match. Catherine was the daughter of a reprobate earl. The father's pursuit of pleasure and the mother's early death had allowed the girl more freedom than was customary. Frail and pale, simple in almost all her tastes, and of exquisitely pure expression, Catherine could have passed for an angel if she had chosen discretion. But Catherine did not choose. And her behaviour was frequently discussed, in raffish circles with knowledge and appreciation, in polite ones with imagination and distaste. Fortified by birth and fortune, Catherine herself was able to ignore opinion up to a point, and seemed to rise from each debauch purer and whiter than before.

Their refinements of sensuality persuaded the young Jew that he loved the girl. Each was perhaps a little dazzled by the incandescence they achieved together, and the lover naturally wounded when, at what might have been thought the height of the affair, his mistress was discovered in a hotel bedroom with an Indian prince. For the first time Catherine must have sensed the narrowness of the plank she was treading, for it became known almost at once that she had gone abroad, for an indefinite period, with an aunt.

Her lover did receive a letter from Florence:

> My darling M.,
> I wonder whether you will ever be able to forgive me the shatter-ing mistake I caused you to make. I do not expect it. I expect very little of anyone, realizing how little may be expected of myself. But would like to act sentimental, on such a wet night, in this stuffy little town, full of English Ladies Living Abroad. I might feel des-perate, if I had not learnt you off by heart, and were not still able to bring you close, in spite of the revulsion I know the actuality would produce in you. . . .

The letter continued in somewhat literary strain, about the "little green hills of Tuscany, with their exciting undertones of sensuous brown," but he had no inclination to read any farther. He tossed the ball into the basket and loosened his tie. He did not see Catherine again, although from time to time he read about her. She continued to lead a life in accordance with the conventions of her temperament: in her maturity she was almost strangled by a boxer in a mews in Pimlico, and died old, during a bombing raid of the Second War, in a home for inebriates at Putney.

As for Mordecai, he now returned to his studies, with a rage that belonged to youth, and an austerity that he had inherited from his mother, until, shortly after destroying the distasteful letter from his mistress, he received another, of a far more disturbing nature, from his father:

> My dear son,
> I can no longer postpone informing you of the momentous decision I have been forced to make. To come at once to the point: I had been receiving instruction for some time past from a priest of the Roman Catholic Church, and was baptized, I am happy to be able to tell you, last Thursday afternoon. A weight is lifted off my mind.

For the first time in my life, I feel myself truly to be free. *I am a Christian!*

After a lifetime spent studying the Jewish problem, it seems to me that this is the only solution of it. I hardly like to write *practical* solution, but that is the word which came into my mind. To give so little, and receive so much! Because it must be obvious to all but fools that the advantages of every kind are enormous. However, as one who has the fate of our people sincerely at heart, I do not wish to stress those advantages, only to pray that many more of us repent of our stubborn, fruitless ways.

You, Martin, I have felt for some time, are undergoing a crisis in faith. All the more likely, then, that reason may lead you into the right and safe path, when you are ready to decide. It is your dear mother for whom I fear there is little hope. She will choose to remain caught forever in the thicket of Jewish self-righteousness, and the reasonable step I have taken will only continue to cause her pain. Still, I shall pray that some miracle will unite our two souls at last.

I will not trouble you with details of our business house—it is, besides, the summer season—nor shall I introduce comments on the international situation into a communication which is probably, in itself, a source of surprise, and, possibly, dear boy, distress.

I shall remain always
Your affectionate father . . .

Mordecai had never felt emptier than on finishing reading his father's letter. If he himself had dried up, there had always been the host of others, and particularly parents, who remained filled with the oil and spices of tradition. And now his father's phial was broken; all the goodness was run out. One corner of memory might never be revisited.

All through this phase of private desolation, the young Jew forced himself to go about his business, although his associates frequently suspected him of watching somebody else, who stood unseen behind their backs. Of the letters he composed to his apostate father, he sent the one that least conveyed his feelings, and must have caused a pang of disappointment in the recipient. For the letter was indifferent, not to say feeble, in the reactions it expressed.

Of his mother, Mordecai did not dare think, nor did he mention his father's act in the letter he immediately wrote to her.

It did seem for the first time that his own brilliantly inviolable destiny was threatened, by an increased shrivelling of the spirit in himself, as well as by the actions of those whom he had considered almost as statues in a familiar park. Now the statues had begun to move. Great fissures were beginning to appear, besides, in what he had assumed to be the solid mass of history. Time was no longer congealed, but flowing. Some of the young man's acquaintances had already packed their bags. They reminded him that war must come, and that, as a German, it was his duty to return with them before it was too late, to serve the Fatherland.

Scarcely Jew, and scarcely German, Himmelfarb was still debating when he received the letter from his mother:

> My dearest Mordecai,
> Your father will have written you some account of what I cannot bring myself to mention. You will see that I am at present with my sisters, where I shall remain until I have recovered from my loss. They are very kind, considerate, more than I deserve.
> Oh, Mordecai, I can only think I have failed him in some way, and dread that I may also fail my son.

Mordecai averted his face. He could not bear to see his mother. It was as though she had not survived the rending of the garment.

The letter did, at least, release her son from the doldrums of indecision. Very soon Mordecai found himself adrift on the North Sea. Ostensibly he was returning home. So far his will had supported him, but only so far. That which his pride had begun to represent as a steel cable, was, in fact, a thread, which other people cruelly jerked, tangled with their clumsy fingers, and even threatened to break. So the sea air wandered in and out of that insubstantial cabin formed by the young man's bones. His once handsome skin had lost its tone of ivory to a dirty yellow-grey. Those of his fellow passengers who addressed him soon moved away across the deck, sensing a situation with which their own mediocrity could not deal, of hallucination, or perhaps even madness. A few, however, plumped for a simpler explanation: the damned Jew was drunk.

Drunk or sober, he arrived at Holunderthal with admirable punctuality. Inside the skeleton of the station, the faces of strangers appeared convinced of their timelessness. Only his father, in his dark, correct coat, admitted age. His moustache was fumbling with a welcome. Or some undue perplexity. The young man's Aunt Zipporah, his mother's sister, a woman he had always disliked, for a certain smell of poverty, and association with disaster, spoke to him out of a strained throat.

The aunt and the father were making way for each other.

"Yes," said Mordecai. "We had the kind of crossing one expects."
And waited.

"Tell me," he said finally. "It is my mother."
And listened.

The aunt began to cry, like a rat that has been caught at last. Trapped inside the girders of Holunderthal *Hauptbahnhof,* it sounded awful. Inquisitive passers-by slowed down, and waited for a revelation to dictate their proper attitude.

"Yes!" cried his Aunt Zipporah. "Your mother. On Saturday night. But over quickly, Mordecai."

His father had begun to nail him with his voice.

"It appears there was some internal malady she had been hiding from us, Mordecai."

The aunt's grief gushed afresh.

"Oÿ-yoÿ-yoÿ! Moshe! There was no malignancy. I have it from Dr Ehrenzweig. Not the least trace of a malignancy."

Such luxuriant grief made that of her brother-in-law sound mercilessly arid. But his desperation was of a different kind.

"Dr Ehrenzweig assures me," he insisted, "that she did not suffer. No pain, Mordecai. Up to the end."

"Did not suffer! Did not suffer!" The aunt's voice blew and flapped. "There are different ways of suffering! Dr Ehrenzweig was responsible only for his patient's body."

The father had seized his son by an elbow.

"This woman is vindictive, because, naturally, she is biased!" Moshe shouted.

The fact was, Mordecai knew, his mother had, simply, died.

So they walked on, and into a *Droschke,* over the heads of half-a-dozen carnations, which some other traveller had discarded, on finding them, perhaps, unbearable.

For the few weeks before the outbreak of war, young Himmelfarb remained in his father's house. The father brought presents to lay at his son's feet, without, however, finding forgiveness. The son resumed relations with relations, with the community who had received him at *bar mitzvah,* for, officially, he was still a Jew. But the voices of the elders would threaten to dry up as he approached, and upon his entering a room, young, modest girls would lower their eyes and blush. He accepted that he was an outcast. He only failed to realize that neither his father's apostasy nor his own spiritual withdrawal was the true cause of their suspicion, and that almost every soul must endure the same period of probation before receiving orders.

Of gentile friendships, none remained. Jürgen Stauffer was reined in somewhere, waiting to ride across Europe; nor did Martin-Mordecai care to visualize his friend's face, its adolescence pared away to the bones of manhood, the chivalry of *Minnesinger* translated into *Wille zur Macht* in the expression of the mackerel eyes. Stauffer the publisher had died of a heart, Mordecai was told; his wife had become involved in a prolonged and unpredictable middle age. Only the elder son appeared once, briefly, under a hat, in the doorway of a tram. It was obvious Konrad Stauffer did not remember, or else he had decided not to. The face had adopted an expression of deliberate boorishness, which did not altogether convince. Himmelfarb had heard that Stauffer was the author of a volume of poems, which nobody had read, and that he was now writing destructive reviews and articles for a radical newspaper in their home town.

But soon the image of Stauffer was swallowed up, together with the past, and that part of his life which Himmelfarb had dared to call his own. War did not come as a surprise, to him, or anyone, that is, it did not erupt in the manner of volcanoes, it seeped over and into them. Some were appalled at the prospect of their becoming involved, but many sang, as if welcoming a lover, one who might certainly crack their ribs and bruise their flesh, but whose saliva intoxicated as it poisoned, and whose passion liberated their more inadmissible desires.

Because the sequence of events in his personal life had left him sceptical and cold, war, his first too, affected Himmelfarb less than might have been expected. At the height of its folly, he was ashamed to realize, it was taking place only on the edge of his consciousness. However, as a good German, he had volunteered, and was accepted to serve in the infantry. He was wounded twice. He even won a medal.

Once, in the mud and rain of a ruined French village, he enjoyed the half-pleasure of encountering his former friend Jürgen Stauffer. The shining lieutenant embraced the rather scruffy Jewish private— the sun was setting, there was nobody about—and, with only a little encouragement, would have risked creating a duet for opera out of their innocent situation.

"Ach, Gott!" cried the *Herr Leutnant.* "Martin! Of all men, my old, my dearest Martin! At sunset! In Treilles! At the end of our victorious advance!"

The Jew wondered how he might clamber after, if only just a little of the way.

"It is heart-warming"—the *Herr Leutnant* could not sing enough— "to renew valued friendships in unexpected places."

Something, certainly, whether skill or conviction, had caused the *Heldentenor* to glow. Cut out of felt and cardboard, his golden skin streaming with last light, he maintained the correct position, as they stood together in the shambles of a street. He smelled, moreover, his tired inferior realized, of boot polish and toilet soap.

"But how are you, Martin? You don't tell me," the officer complained in different key.

The approach of caution had caused him to moisten unnecessarily his glistening lips.

"I am well," answered the Jew. "That is, my arches have fallen."

How Jürgen Stauffer roared. His teeth were perfect.

"Still a joker! My good Martin! But keep your health. We are almost there."

"Where?" asked the Jew.

The officer waved his hand. His brilliance could make allowances for the impudence of simplicity. So he forgave, still laughingly, still glancing back, over his shoulder as well as into the past, at some extraordinary misjudgment on his own part, as he walked away through the mud to rejoin a general who depended on his company.

Peace is sometimes more explosive than war. So it seemed to many of those who lived through what followed: rootling after sausage-ends and the heads of sour herrings, expressing in their songs a joy they no longer possessed, forced by hunger and the need for warmth into erotic situations their parents would not have guessed at.

Swimming and sinking, trampling and trampled, the rout of men-animals was carried along, and with them the Jew Himmelfarb. If he ever experienced the will to resist, he never exercised it, and even derived comfort from the friction of similar bristles on his own. During the first weeks of release, strange embraces, a delirium of experience, prevented him from returning to the bed that was, of course, waiting for him in his father's house. Besides, in those surroundings he might have laughed too loud, or farted in the

dining-room, or done something of an irrational nature. For Moshe
had remarried. He had taken a young woman called Christel
Schmidt, with hair as heavy and yellow in its snood as horses' dung,
and the necklace of Venus on her neck. *Trotzdem, nett und tüchtig.*
And of no further significance. The lovers had met after mass. The
girl consented, partly out of curiosity, but more especially because
she could not bear to feel hungry. As for the old man, any flicker
of prudence was probably extinguished by visions of a last frenzy
of consenting flesh.

Mordecai and his practically innocent stepmother were both
relieved to put an end to an ironic situation when, after months, the
former was appointed to a readership in English at the University
of Bienenstadt. Dr Himmelfarb departed, with the tentative
blessings of his old father, and an inkling that he had been directed to this far from lucrative post at a minor university for reasons still obscure. Several homely Jews insisted on offering him
introductions to others, probably of their own kind, which he accepted with amused gratitude, and on a street corner, the disgusting
dyer of his youth clawed at his arm and repeated, it seemed, end-
lessly:

"There is a good man at Bienenstadt, a printer, a cousin of my
late wife's brother-in-law. This man will receive you with lovingkindness, such as you were accustomed to in childhood, I need not
remind you, Herr Mordecai. I recommend him to you with all my
heart. His name is Liebmann."

Dr Himmelfarb could not escape quickly enough from the grip
of the dyer, who continued to call after him, "An excellent man!
Lieb-mann is the name!"

He might have begun to spell it out, if somebody impatient had
not pushed him into the gutter.

Soon after, Himmelfarb left for Bienenstadt.

The town itself was in many ways similar to the one in which
he had been born, smaller certainly, but illuminated by the same
brush. Its blue and grey, and flecks of weathered gilding, swam
together in a midday sleep. Words trickled from the mouths of the
inhabitants in an untainted stream. Faces dimpled with a professional friendliness, and a conviction that only they could ever be
right. Yet, at Bienenstadt, Himmelfarb was soothed by the drone of
days, even by the tone of its hypocrisies. Of his students, most

obeyed his commands with the respect of earnest youth; a few, even, seemed of the opinion that he had more than knowledge to offer, and would loiter in hot silence, when lectures were done, as if hoping for some revelation of a personal kind.

It was not that he was loved, exactly, but he could have been, if he had not withdrawn for the moment too far into himself to be reached. He had torn up all those introductions forced on him by acquaintances before his departure from Holunderthal, for he felt that to use them might have proved laughable or boring. He kept to his room a good deal, and read Spengler late at night.

Months had passed before he began to be tormented by a name, for which he could not at first account. It became a source of irritation, like somebody tapping out the same phrase repeatedly on a buzzer. He would even find the name on his tongue. Then he remembered: it was that of the dreadful dyer's Bienenstadt relative. Which made the whole business more ridiculous and irritating than before. He had no intention of forming any such connection. As soon as he was aware of its origin, he laughed the smoke out of his lungs whenever the name recurred. He would light a fresh cigarette. His fingers, he noticed, were growing stained. And trembled slightly.

Then quite suddenly, on a certain afternoon, he stood up knowing that he must go in search of Liebmann the printer. He could not have been more relieved, not to say elated, as he heard his feet clatter on the cobbles in the older part of the town. His wingèd hair, too luxuriant by standards of elegance and worldliness, floated in the light breeze.

So he arrived at the house. He had chosen an hour, towards evening, when the printer's business affairs would surely have released him. Certainly the ground floor was still, deserted, padlocked. In a lane at the side he discovered a door, which could have communicated with the actual dwelling. Yes, said the between-age girl who came; but her father was not yet back from the synagogue. After a pause for her instincts to debate, she told him he should come in, and led him by the stairs to where the family lived above the press. He was brought into a room in which the shutters had been pushed back, and a young woman was examining what appeared to be a paper-knife, which she had just unwrapped from a parcel.

"Oh, yes! Israel!" she said, and laughed, after the visitor left by her sister had made some reference to the dyer. "We have not seen him for years. I cannot remember when."

She might have made a face, if kindness had not prevented her. Instead, she showed him the paper-knife she had just received. "From a cousin," she explained, "who has returned from Janina. But I shall have no uses for it," she regretted, and now she did make the face, and it looked most comical. "Who but a stage duchess ever used a real paper-knife to cut books or open letters?"

Their combined laughter was unnaturally loud.

"Surely there are other uses?" suggested the visitor, still laughing.

"Oh, yes. Undoubtedly," agreed the girl. "It is so *sharp!*"

With the point of the knife she pricked the ball of one of her thumbs, which grew quite white, and caused them to laugh more brilliantly than ever.

Then they were both ashamed, because they had never behaved like this before. It was unnatural to both of them.

But exhilarating. Each was breathless.

The girl began to talk again.

"Yes, my father will come soon," she said, but incidentally. "Then we shall have some coffee. I am the eldest. I am Reha." After which, she reeled off the names of several brothers and sisters. "Didn't Israel tell you about the family? Of course, he scarcely knows us. No, my mother is dead."

It was a big, old-fashioned room in one of the gabled houses.

"You will think I am an awful chatterbox," she said, pushing back some hair. "The others always shout me down. Do you like it here? I mean, at Bienenstadt?"

"Yes," he said. "I suppose I like it."

"Tell me what you do," she invited.

So he did, altogether naturally now.

Reha was a plump and rather dowdy girl. It was already evident how comfortable she would eventually become, and happy, if it were to be permitted. In looking at her, Himmelfarb was compelled to hold his head on one side, in a manner quite new to him, an attempt at delicacy perhaps. She did not invite attentions, let alone courtship, and had that rather homely face, yet he found himself trying to please, without expecting rewards, continually anxious lest some too florid gesture, or elaboration of thought, might convey pretentiousness where sincerity had been intended.

"English," she murmured, frowningly. "My vocabulary was always weak. I did not force myself to read enough."

"I shall lend you books," he promised.

Each was conscious of the classic obviousness of their remarks, but it did not seem to matter.

The father came in. He was a thin, small old Jew, with a game leg, and perhaps some secret ailment, or it could have been that he had never fully recovered from the death of his wife. When he heard how the visitor was sent, he came out of himself, however, and repeated several times, "Poor Israel! Poor Israel!"

In a tone of voice which suggested that the hopelessness of his relative's case might have endowed him with a virtue.

"In spite of his name, I must tell you, Israel is childless. Some early misfortune," the printer continued, without stopping to consider how well informed his visitor might be. "But has devoted himself to other matters. The seed can be sown, you know, in many ways."

It was clear the printer would have preferred to withdraw again into himself, but he remarked quite spontaneously, and with a dry courtesy, "I hope you will always come to us on the Sabbath, sir. Make this your home. There are passages in the Books I would like to discuss with you. I would like to hear your opinion of the general situation."

However formally the suggestion was presented, the printer's yellow skin remained tinged with the faint glow of lovingkindness. The eyes were too innocent to avoid entering those of his fellow men, with the result that Himmelfarb was forced to lower his own, while hoping that his host's goodness might prevent him from recognizing the disorder which prevailed within.

The printer was saying, "There are many problems that you may illuminate for us, Dr Himmelfarb. We live inside a closed circle. That is our great weakness."

If the visitor had not contracted the muscles of his throat with all his strength, he might have startled his grave host by shouting a denial. That, at least, was prevented.

After some further conversation, he saw that Reha had returned with coffee. She was standing looking in distress and surprise at what, he realized, was the knot of his hands. But he released them quickly. The white vanished from his knuckles. And at once she made it appear doubtful whether she had noticed. She was pouring the coffee, inclining and smiling in the slight steam. It certainly smelled of real, pre-war coffee. And there were wedges of *Käsekuchen* besides.

Himmelfarb went to Liebmanns' on the Sabbath, as had been suggested. He was diffident about it at first, but longing supported him, and soon it became a habit. As the whole family appeared to take his presence for granted, it seemed at last, to him too, perfectly natural. When they handed him the Sabbath dishes at table, or expected him to join in their songs, it was assumed that his life as a Jew had never been interrupted. Sometimes his happiness was an embarrassment to him. But nobody noticed, unless Ari.

Ari, the eldest boy, was probably a specialist in scenting out other people's secrets, certainly their weaknesses. Bullet-headed in his *Käppchen,* he had whorls of dark hair along his cheekbones. He would mumble a grace through his broad, goat's teeth, eyes half-closed, almost smiling.

In the synagogue Ari once turned to Mordecai, and did not even bother to whisper.

"See that fellow over there? The one with the locks. He is so simple—that is to say, he is such a *good Jew* that, if his grandfather stuck on a mask, and told Abram he was Elijah the Prophet, he would believe it."

Ari did not expect Mordecai to laugh, but laughed for himself. He was perfectly detached. But he was not a bad lad. He would go off tramping and singing across the *Heide* with other young Jews, members of an organization to which he belonged. He loved his family, too, and would sit at table with his arms round his sisters' necks.

Mordecai believed that, in time, he might even love Ari. Of the Sabbath table, he loved the crusts. The crumbs beneath his fingers humbled him.

"What is it?" Reha might ask. "Don't you like the carp? Or is it, perhaps, the *Biersosse?*"

In the silence after his reassurance, she would fidget with her plate. And look for something. Like his mother, she was myopic. In the beginning Reha had not been able to resist joking with their guest about the blind leading the blind, for Himmelfarb, as it turned out, had inherited indifferent sight, and shortly before his arrival at Bienenstadt, had been forced to take to spectacles. These sat somewhat oddly on his face, and might have weakened its natural defences if they had not been reinforced by an expression of increasing certainty.

For the young man who was no longer a stranger, the Sabbath became a steadfast joy, whether sitting in the twilight of the printer's house, or, at the synagogue, touching elbows with his friend Liebmann, as they stood wrapped in their trailing shawls. As the coverings of the Ark were changed, in accordance with the feasts of the year, so his soul would put on different colours. He was again furnished with his faith. To touch the fringes of his shawl with his lips, was to drink pure joy.

In autumn, when the heat had passed, he sometimes persuaded Reha Liebmann, who was secretly appalled by open spaces, to go walking with him through the barren heathland which stretched to the north of Bienenstadt, and, on a Sunday in October, as they sat and rested in a sandy, slightly more protected hollow, he suggested she should become his wife.

She would not answer at first, by any word, but was separating the grains of sand, and could have been sad, or bitter.

To tell the truth, it surprised the vanity in him, but only for a moment.

She did begin, very slowly, very softly.

"Yes," she said. "Yes, Mordecai. I had been hoping. From the beginning I had been hoping. But knew, too, of course."

If her words had lacked simplicity, such candour might have sounded complacent, or even immodest.

"Oh, dear!" She began to cry. "I must try very hard. Forgive me," she cried. "That I should behave like this. Just now. I am afraid I may fail you also in other ways."

"Reha, darling!" he answered rather lightly. "In the eyes of the world a provincial intellectual is a *comic* figure."

"Ah, but you do not understand," she managed with difficulty. "Not yet. And I cannot express myself. But we—some of us—although we have not spoken—know that you will bring us honour."

She took his fingers, and was looking absently, again almost sadly, at their roots. She stroked the veins in the backs of his hands.

"You make me ashamed," he protested.

Because he was astounded.

"You will see," she said. "I am convinced."

And looked up, smiling confidently now.

So that he wanted to kiss her—she was so good and tangible—but at the same time he was determined to forget the strange, rather hysterical assertions his proposal had inspired.

"Reha! Reha! If you only knew!" he insisted. "I am the lowest of human beings!"

But it did not deter her from taking his head in her arms. It was as though she would possess it for as long as one is allowed to possess anything in this world. Yet she did so with humility, conscious of the minor part she would be given to play.

When at last they got to their feet, after comforting each other by words and touch, they were amazed and shy. The bronze trumpets were calling their names, in that remote and rather sour hollow of the *Heide,* as evening fell.

Soon the days were tumbling over one another, babbling in the accents of old women, younger sisters and girl cousins, until the bridegroom was standing beneath the *chuppah,* waiting for his bride. She came very softly, as might have been expected, like a breath. Then the two were standing together, but no longer bound by their awkward bodies, under the canopy of stuffy velvet, in the particular smell of sanctity and scouring of the old synagogue at Bienenstadt, in an assembly of tradesmen and small shopkeepers, who were the seed of Israel fallen on that corner of Germany. The miraculous, encrusted *chuppah* did actually open for the chosen couple; they were sucked out of themselves into an infinity of blue, and their souls were flapping together, diffidently at first, as two handkerchiefs will flutter and dispute each other's form and direction in a wind, until, reconciled by nature to the truth of the situation, they reach out, wrapped together, straining always higher, in one strong, white tongue.

So the souls of the united couple temporarily abandoned their surroundings, while the bodies of bridegroom and bride continued to stand beneath the canopy, enacting the touching and simple ceremonies in which the congregation might participate. How the old men and women craned to distinguish the gold circlet that the young man was slipping on the bride's finger. The old, dusty men and women were again encircled by love and history. Their own lips tasted joyful wine, and trembled to forestall the breaking of the cup.

For the bridegroom had taken the glass, as no happiness can be repeated, all must be relived, resanctified. So the bridegroom stood with the glass poised. It was unbearably perfect, immaculate, but fragile. It was already breaking—breaking—broken. During a second of silence, its splinters glittered on the brick floor.

There were, of course, a few present who had broken into tears for the destruction of the glass, but even they joined with the congregation in shouting with joy, all, out of the depths of their hearts. They were truly overjoyed by that which they had just enacted together. Hope was renewed in everybody. "Mazel tov!" cried the toothless mouths of the old people, and the red, shrilly voices of the young girls vibrated with hysteria and anticipation.

Only the bridegroom seemed to have entered on another phase. He appeared almost morose, as he stood fidgeting beneath the now grotesque and brooding chuppah. Time had, in fact, carried him too far too fast, with the result that the beard had sprouted again on his shaven jaw, and as he dipped his chin, thoughtful and frowning, the neck of the white kittel which protruded unevenly above his wedding jacket was chafing against the bristles of incipient beard. So he frowned, and bit one end of his moustache, and heard the first delicately staged message of falling earth which precedes the final avalanche of mortality.

Afterwards, at the house of the father-in-law, Mordecai was whirled around and around so often, to receive embraces or advice, that the thinking man succumbed temporarily to the sensual one. Without listening to much of what he was told, he laughed back out of his parted, swelling lips, quite unlike himself. And rubbed his eyes occasionally to rid them of the blur of candles. Always laughing rather than replying. The air, besides, was unctuous with a smell of goose fat and the steam from golden soup.

In the mood of relaxed sensuality which the wedding feast had induced, it did not strike him as tragic that there were none of his own present. Tactfully, his father had developed a severe chill, which kept him confined to his bed. His aunts, self-engrossed and ailing women, had never really recovered from the circumstances of their sister's death. But one figure did emerge from the past, and when he had put his arms round the bridegroom, Mordecai recognized the dyer from Holunderthal.

"I did not doubt you would see what was indicated," slobbered the awful man into the bridegroom's ear. "And know you will justify our expectations. Because your heart has been touched and changed."

The guests were swarming around, and jostling them, so that Mordecai only succeeded with difficulty in holding the dyer off by handfuls of the latter's scurfy coat.

"Touched and changed?" He laughed back, and heard it sound faintly stupid. "I am, as always, myself, I regret to tell you!"

"That is so, and that is why!" the dyer replied.

Pressed together as they were, Mordecai realized that the man's hitherto sickly body had a warmth and strength he would never have suspected. Nor was he himself half as disgusted as he had been on previous occasions, though now, of course, he had taken several glasses of wine.

"But you are all riddles—secrets!" In spite of their proximity it was necessary to shout to be heard above the noise.

"There is no secret," the dyer appeared to be saying, or shouting back. "Equanimity is no secret. Solitariness is no secret. True solitariness is only possible where equanimity exists. An unquiet spirit can introduce distractions into the best-prepared mind."

"But this is immoral!" Mordecai protested, shouting. "And on such an occasion! It is a denial of community. Man is not a hermit."

"Depending on the man, he is a light that will reflect out over the community—all the brighter from a bare room."

As they were practically bellowing at each other, nobody else had heard, which was perhaps just as well, and at that moment they were separated by the printer, who wanted to display his son-in-law to some acquaintance or relative.

As his self-appointed guide was sucked back into the crowd and lost, Himmelfarb accepted that the crippled dyer, who had come even to the wedding with the lines of his hands marked clearly in purple, was one from whom he would never escape. He had learnt the shape of the unshapely body, the texture of the unchanging coat;

mirrors had taught him, long before their meeting, the expression of the eyes. Now, in the moment of perception, all the inklings were married together: the dyer's image was with him for always, like his new wife, or his own fate. Now he was committed. So he continued to answer distractedly the questions of the wedding guests, while trying to reconcile in his mind what his wife had taught him of love, with what had hitherto been the disgust he had felt for the dyer. In the light of the one, he must discover and gather up the sparks of love hidden in the other. Or deny his own purpose, as well as the existence of the race.

In the circumstances, he was amazed nobody realized the answers they were receiving to their questions were no answers, or that his wife Reha should look up at him with an expression of implicit confidence.

In the beginning the young people lived with the wife's father, but soon found, and moved into, a small, rather old-fashioned house, with rooms high but too narrow, and a very abrupt staircase. Because it was situated on the outskirts of the town, at least the rental was low, which enabled the tenants to engage an inexperienced girl to help the wife of the *Dozent,* while the *Dozent* himself gave up smoking, and practised other small economies such as walking to his lectures instead of taking the tram. They were completely happy, the female relatives claimed, and indeed, they were almost so. In their small, closed circle. On the outskirts of the town. Those who look for variety in change and motion, instead of in the variations on recurring events, would have found the life monotonous and restricted. But Himmelfarbs gave no outward sign of wishing to diverge from the path on which their feet had been set. If they left Bienenstadt at all, it was to spend the same month each year in the *Schwarzwald,* at the same reliable pension where it was possible to eat kosher. Although there were also occasions when Dr Himmelfarb had had to absent himself for several days, representing a disinclined professor at conferences in other university towns. And once, after some years, he had returned to Holunderthal, on receiving a telegram announcing the death of his father.

Moshe died of his young wife, it was commonly and truthfully said. But repentant. That is easy at the end. And was buried by a priest with a stammer, and an acolyte with a cold. The few friends

who attended were sufficiently recent to keep the ceremony superficial in tone. Most of the faces were kindly, curious, reverent, correct, but a few who were bored, or who suffered from bad circulation, took to stamping ostentatiously, or slapping their sides, and
one more cynical than the rest reflected how quickly a mild joke
can become a stale one. All of these were anxious to get finished.
But each clod had to count. As they summoned the Mother of God
to the side of an old Jew, who had not known Her very long, and
then, it was suspected, only as a convenience. So the earth was
scattered, and water—though not of tears, not even from the son,
whose grief was deeper than the gush of tears.

The son, who had gone round to the wrong side of the grave,
amongst the earth and stones, and who had no idea what to do by
way of respect, stood looking yellow in the silver afternoon. Some
of the mourners grew quite fascinated, if repelled, by his pronounced
Jewish cast.

As they watched, Mordecai swayed from time to time. Because
the weight was upon him. Because faith is never faith unless it is to
be wrestled with. *O perfect Rock, spare and have pity on the parents and the children.* . . . So Mordecai wrestled with the Rock,
and prayed for his parent, that shifting sand, or worldly man, whose
moustache had smelt deliciously, and who had never been happier
than when presenting a Collected Works in leather.

Himmelfarb remained no longer than was necessary in his native town. Fortunately the business had been satisfactorily disposed
of a couple of years before. The widow, who was already preparing
to forget about that chapter of her life, proposed to look for consolation at a foreign spa. There remained the house on the Holzgraben,
which the son inherited, and decided to close until a suitable tenant
could be found. He was most anxious to return as quickly as possible to the life he had made, and which his increase in fortune proceeded to alter only in superficial ways, for his wife could never
accustom herself to worldly practices, and he remained engrossed in
her, his students, and his books.

It was not generally known in Bienenstadt that Dr Himmelfarb
himself had written and published an admirable and scholarly little
monograph on the *Novels of John Oliver Hobbes.* Although the
Frau Doktor had made a point of mentioning the fact casually to
the ladies of her circle, the information was not absorbed. Why

should it have been? The book would remain a scholar's minor achievement, or, at most, an object of interest to some research student exploring the byways of literature. However, his large-scale work, *English Novelists of the Nineteenth Century in Relation to German Literature and Life*, also written during the quiet years at Bienenstadt, was rather a different matter. Himmelfarb's *English Novelists* attracted a wider academic, not to say public attention, and it was taken for granted that the author would soon be generally accepted as a standard authority. So that, before very long, there was an outbreak of smiling discussion amongst the ladies of the *Frau Doktor*'s circle, of the rumours they had heard: how Dr Himmelfarb was likely to be offered the Chair of English at a certain university—gossip was in disagreement over which; perhaps *Frau Doktor* Himmelfarb—here the ladies of the circle wreathed themselves in golden smiles—might be able to enlighten them. But, when questioned on that matter of advancement, the *Frau Doktor* would look rather nervous, as if she had been asked to tamper with the future. She personally preferred to await the logical unfolding of events, which her husband's brilliance must ensure.

So she would avoid giving a direct reply. Or she would murmur something of tried banality, such as, "All in good time. Our lives have only just begun."

And offer her callers a second slice of *Käsekuchen*.

In a sense, no more rational answer could have been found, for, although the *Dozent* was turning grey—not unnatural in a man of dark pigmentation—and his fine figure had begun to thicken, while his wife had grown undeniably fat, it could have been argued that they were only beginning to mature in the full goodness of their married lives. In the small house on the outskirts of the town. In the shade of an oak, and the lesser shadows of beans, which the industrious country maid had coaxed to climb up sticks in the back garden. Nobody, least of all Himmelfarbs themselves, could really have wished to destroy the impression of peaceful permanence, strongest always in the mornings, when the feather-beds lolled in the sunlight on the upper window-sills.

Yet, Frau Himmelfarb began to suffer from breathlessness, which gave her, when off her guard, a slightly strained look, as if her assertion of happiness might be proving too difficult to maintain. Some of her callers, in discussing it, decided it was the proximity of the oak—too many trees round a house used up all the oxygen, causing those spasms which, in the end, might turn to asthma; while other ladies, more daring, were of the opinion that the absence of a family had provoked a nervous condition.

One of the latter, a gross creature by intellectual standards, whose husband was a haberdasher in a mean street, and who was received on account of a relationship, knew no better than to say outright, "But, Rehalein, it is time you had a child. Why, the duties of the *rabbanim* do not begin and end in books. Give me a good, comfortable, family Jew. He may not spell, but he will fill the house with babies."

Two other ladies, one of whom was noted for her readings from the *West-Östlicher Diwan,* decided it was time to break off even forced relations with the haberdasher's wife, who was smelling, besides, of perspiration and caraway seeds.

While Reha Himmelfarb simply maintained, "Who are we, Rifke, to decide what a man's duties shall be?"

And Himmelfarb loved his wife the better for overhearing.

They were brought together closer, if anything, in an effort to express that love of which it seemed no lasting evidence might remain. None would know how Himmelfarbs had rejoiced in each other, unless by an echo from a library, from the dedication in a book: *To my Wife, Reha, without whose encouragement and assistance . . .* But words do not convince the doubting soul like living tokens, as the wife of the haberdasher knew, for all her simplicity, or perhaps because of it.

Watching his wife one evening as she lit the Sabbath candles, Himmelfarb would have said: Of all people in this world, Reha is least in doubt. Yet, at that moment, the hands of Reha Himmelfarb, plump and practical by nature, seemed to grow transparent, and flicker in the candle flames.

At the same time she gave a little startled cry of pain.

"It was the wax from the candles! The hot wax, that fell when I was not expecting."

She whispered quickly, and only just distinct, as though she felt her need to explain desecrate a sacred moment.

By then the flames of the candles were standing straight and still, but what should have been the lovely, limpid Sabbath light shone wan and almost sickly, and the faces of the two people reflected by the mirrors could have been soft, sweating wax.

The obligations of other ceremonies prevented him from commenting there and then, but later he came to her, and said, "Reha, darling, I can tell you are badly disappointed."

And took her resisting hand, and put it inside his jacket, so that it was closest to him.

"Why?" she cried. "When our life together is so happy? And soon there will be the Chair. Everybody is convinced of that."

He was half exasperated, half in love.

"But not the babies that your Cousin Rifke advises as the panacea."

She would not look at him. She said, "We must expect our lives to be different."

"Referring in cold abstractions," he answered, "to matters we do not understand. But for our actual lives—for yours, at least—I would ask all that is comforting and joyous."

"Oh, mine!" she protested. "I am nothing. I am your footstool. Or cushion!" She laughed. "Am I not, rather, a cushion?"

She did appear her plumpest looking up at him, happy even, but, he suspected, by her own effort.

Then she put her arms round his waist, and laid her face against his vest, and said, "I would not alter a single detail of our lives."

But at once went on to deliver, in a different voice, what sounded almost a recitative, of the greatest significance and urgency, "On Monday I must start to make the jelly from the apples Mariechen brought from her village. There is an old book my mother used to mention, which gives an infallible method for clarifying jelly. I have the title, I believe, amongst some papers she left. Pass by Rutkowitz's, on your way home, and see whether you can find the book. Will you, Mordecai? He has such a mountain of old stuff, you might come across anything."

She looked up, and was in such apparent earnest, he was both moved and pacified.

On the Monday, as he was preparing to leave, Reha came with the title of the book. As it happened, he had forgotten.

"Don't forget the book!" she kept insisting. "I shall not start the jelly. I shall wait in case you happen to find. At Rutkowitz's. The book!"

It was so important, her face implied.

Then he left, relieved that his wife was such a simple, loving creature. If her words sometimes hinted at deeper matters, no doubt it was pure chance; she herself remained unaware.

Rutkowitz was a quiet, elderly Jew, whose overflowing shop stood in one of the streets which plunged off behind the university at Bienenstadt. Himmelfarb remembered to pass that way before returning home, and rummaged in the stacks and trays for the book his wife so particularly required. Needless to say, he did not succeed in finding it, but discovered other things which amused and interested.

"You deal in magic, Rutkowitz, I see!"

Deliberately he addressed the grave bookseller with inappropriate levity.

The latter shrugged, and answered, very dry, "Some old cabalistic and Hasidic works. They came from a collection in Prague."

"And are of value?"

"There are some who may value them."

The bookseller was a wary man.

Himmelfarb warmed to the characters, and the language moved on his tongue, where the Cantor Katzmann had put it in the beginning. He began, inevitably, to read aloud, for the nostalgia of hearing the instrument of his voice do justice to its heritage.

And so, he heard:

> "I set myself the task at night of combining letters with one another, and of meditating on them, and so continued for three nights. On the third occasion, after midnight, I nodded off for a little, quill in hand, paper on my knees. Then I noticed that the candle was about to go out. So I rose and extinguished it, as a person who has been dozing often will. But I soon realized that the light continued. I was greatly astonished, because, after close examination, I saw it was as though the light issued from myself. I said: 'I do not believe it.' I walked to and fro all through the house, and, behold, the light is with me; I lay on a couch and covered myself up, and, behold, the light is with me all the while. . . ."

The cautious bookseller was standing a little to one side, the better to disclaim complicity in his customer's private pursuits.

"Do you appreciate the physical advantages of mystical ecstasy, Rutkowitz?" Himmelfarb inquired.

But although they stood scarcely any distance apart, the bookseller had apparently determined to keep his understanding carefully turned away. He did not answer.

Himmelfarb continued to browse amongst the old books and manuscripts. Now he was entranced. The bookseller had left him, or else had ceased to exist. In the stillness of the dusk and the light from one electric bulb, the reader heard himself:

> "The soul is full of the love of God, and bound with ropes of love, in joy and lightness of heart. Unlike one who serves his master grudgingly, even when most hindered the love of service burns in his heart, and he is glad to fulfil the will of his Creator. . . . For, when the soul thinks deeply on the fear of God, then the flame of heartfelt love leaps within, and the exultation of subtlest joy fills the heart. . . . And the lover dreams not of the advantages of this world; he no longer takes undue pleasure in his wife, nor excessive pride in his sons and daughters, but cares only to obey the will of his Creator, to do good unto others, and to keep sanctified the Name of God. All his thoughts burn with the fire of love for Him. . . ."

Himmelfarb found the bookseller seated at his desk in the lower shop, as though nothing in particular had happened—and what, indeed, had? After coming to an agreement, the *Dozent* went home, taking with him several of the more interesting old volumes of Hebrew, and one or two loose, damaged parchments.

"Did you find my book?"

Reha had appeared in the hall as she heard her husband mounting the stairs.

"No luck!" he answered.

She did not seem in any way put out, but immediately called back into the kitchen, "Mariechen, we shall start the apple jelly tonight. By the old method. The *Herr Doktor* did not find the book."

Almost as though she were relieved.

Her husband continued on his way upstairs. He had debated whether to tell his wife about his purchases, but as she had ignored the books in his arms, he no longer felt he was expected to.

Often now, after correcting an accumulation of essays, or on saying good night to students who had come for tuition, he would sit alone in his room with the old books. He would read, or sit, or draw, idly, automatically, or fidget with different objects, or listen to the sound of silence, and was sometimes, it seemed, transported in divers directions.

On one occasion his wife interrupted.

"I cannot sleep," she explained.

She had released her hair, and brushed it out, with the result that she appeared to be standing against a dark and brittle thicket, but one in which a light shone.

"I am not disturbing you?" she asked. "I thought I would like to read something." She sighed. "Something short. And musical."

"Mörike," he suggested.

"Yes," she agreed, absently. "Mörike will be just the thing."

As the wind her nightdress made in passing stirred the papers uppermost on her husband's desk, she could not resist asking, "What is that, Mordecai? I did not know you could draw."

"I was scribbling," he said. "This, it appears, is the Chariot."

"Ah," she exclaimed, softly, withdrawing her glance; she could have lost interest. "Which chariot?" she did certainly ask, but now it might have been to humour him.

"That, I am not sure," he replied. "It is difficult to distinguish. Just when I think I have understood, I discover some fresh form— so many—streaming with implications. There is the Throne of God, for instance. That is obvious enough—all gold, and chrysoprase, and jasper. Then there is the Chariot of Redemption, much more shadowy, poignant, personal. And the faces of the riders. I cannot begin to see the expression of the faces."

All the time Reha was searching the shelves.

"This is in the old books?" she asked.

"Some of it," he admitted, "is in some."

Reha continued to explore the shelves.

She yawned. And laughed softly.

"I think I shall probably fall asleep," she said, "before I find Mörike."

But took a volume.

He felt her kiss the back of his head as she left.

Or did she remain, to protect him more closely, with some secret part of her being, after the door had closed? He was never certain with Reha: to what extent perception was revealed in her words and her behaviour, or how far she had accompanied him along the inward path.

For, by now, Himmelfarb had taken the path of inwardness. He could not resist silence, and became morose on evenings when he was prevented from retreating early to his room. Reha would continue to sew, or mend. Her expression did not protest. She would smile a gentle approval—but of what, it was never made clear.

Some of the old books were full of directions which he did not dare follow, and to which he adopted a deliberately sceptical attitude, or, if it was ever necessary, one of crudest cynicism. But he did, at last, unknown, it was to be hoped, to his rational self, begin fitfully to combine and permute the Letters, even to contemplate the Names.

It was, however, the driest, the most cerebral approach—when spiritually he longed for the ascent into an ecstasy so cool and green that his own desert would drink the heavenly moisture. Still, his forehead of skin and bone continued to burn with what could have been a circlet of iron. Or sometimes he would become possessed by a rigid coldness of mind, his soul absorbed into the entity of his own upright leather chair, his knuckles carved out of oak.

Mostly he remained at a level where, it seemed, he was inacceptable as a vessel of experience, and would fall asleep, and wake at cockcrow. But once he was roused from sleep, during the leaden hours, to identify a face. And got to his feet, to receive the messenger of light, or resist the dark dissembler. When he was transfixed by his own horror. Of his own image, but fluctuating, as though in fire or water. So that the long-awaited moment was reduced to a reflection of the self. In a distorting mirror. Who, then, could hope to be saved? Fortunately, he was prevented from shouting the blasphemies that occurred to him, because his voice had been temporarily removed. Nor could he inflict on the material forms which surrounded him, themselves the cloaks of spiritual deceit, the damage which he felt compelled to do, for his will had become entangled, and his nails were tearing on the shaggy knots. He could only struggle and sway inside the column of his body. Until he toppled forward, and was saved further anguish by hitting his head on the edge of the desk.

Reha Himmelfarb discovered her husband early that morning. He was still weak and confused, barely conscious, as if he had had a congestive attack of some kind. After recovering from her fright, during which she had tried to warm his hands with her own, and was repeatedly kissing, and crying, and breathing into his cold lips, she ran and telephoned to Dr Vogel, who decided, after an examination, that the *Herr Dozent* was suffering from exhaustion as the result of overwork. The doctor ordered his patient to bed, and for a couple of weeks Himmelfarb saw nobody but his devoted wife. It was very delightful. She read him the whole of *Effi Briest,* and he lay with his eyes closed, barely following, yet absorbing the episodes of that touching, though slightly insipid story. Or perhaps it was his wife's voice which he appreciated most, and which, as it joined the words together with a warm and gentle precision, seemed the voice of actuality.

A second fortnight's leave, granted for convalescence, was spent at a little resort on the Baltic. Grey light and a shiver in the air would only have intensified for Himmelfarb the idyll of impeccable dunes and white timber houses, if it had not been for an incident which occurred at the hotel. They had come down early the first evening into the empty dining-room, where a disenchanted apprentice-waiter sat them at any table. Soon the company began to gather, all individuals of a certain class, of discreetly interchangeable clothes and faces. The greetings were correct. The silence knew what to expect. When something most unexpected, not to say disturbing, happened. A retired colonel, at whose table the new arrivals had been seated, marched to his usual place, seized the paper envelope in which it was customary for a guest to keep his napkin, and after retreating to the hall, passionately yelled at the reception desk that it was not his habit to sit at table with Jews.

Nothing like this had ever happened to Himmelfarbs. They were shaken, trembling even. It was obvious that most of their fellow guests were embarrassed, though one or two had to titter. All necessary apologies were made by the management, but in the circumstances, the newcomers agreed they had no appetite, and left the room after a few spoonfuls of a grey soup. During the night each decided never again to mention the incident to the other, but each was aware that the memory of it would remain. However conciliatory the air of Oststrand became, and however punctiliously, in some cases ostentatiously, the more liberal-minded of their fellow guests bowed to them during the rest of their stay, the little, lapping waves continually revealed a glint of metal, and the cries of sea birds drove the mind into a corner of private melancholy.

Yet, the sea air and early hours restored Dr Himmelfarb's health, and he returned to Bienenstadt with all the necessary strength to attack the immediate future. For soon, those who had been whispering about the *Herr Dozent*'s peculiar breakdown were openly discussing his promotion and departure. He was, in fact, called to an interview at Holunderthal, and shortly after, it was announced that he had been offered, and had accepted, the Chair of English at the university of his home town.

So the couple had plenty to occupy them.

"The books alone are a major undertaking!" Frau Himmelfarb was proud to protest.

"I shall look through them," her husband promised, "and expect I shall find a number that I shan't miss if we leave them behind."

"Oh, I am not complaining!" his wife insisted.

"Then," he replied, with affection rather than in censure, "your intonations do not always convey your feelings."

In the end, all was somehow packed. At a last glance, only the wisps of straw and a few sentimental regrets appeared to linger in the house with narrow rooms on the edge of Bienenstadt.

Professor Himmelfarb, the son of Moshe the furrier, was by now a man of private means, and might have led a life of pomp, if he had been so inclined. But was prevented by a sense of irony, as much as by lack of enthusiasm. They did, certainly, open up the family house on the Holzgraben. However forbidding the façade, in the Greco-German style, with stucco pediment and caryatids, at least the interior preserved a soft down of memories along with the furrier's opulence of taste. In the beginning the *Frau Professor* had been somewhat daunted by the total impact of her establishment and surroundings. For, quite apart from the pressure of monumental furniture, the house faced the more formal, or park side of the *Stadtwald,* with the result that the owners, standing at a first-floor window, looked out over shaven lawns and perfectly distributed gravel, across the beds of tuberous begonias and cockscombs, or down a narrowing *Lindenallee,* lined with discreet discus throwers and modest nymphs, to the deep, bulging, indeterminate masses of the *Wald* proper.

The public setting, however incidental, increased the value and importance of the solemn property, and in the years which followed the migration from Bienenstadt, while an illusion of solidity might still be entertained, it was only his sense of irony which saved Professor Himmelfarb from being impressed by his material condition, in particular when, returning from his walks in the *Wald,* he was confronted with the gradually expanding façade of what was apparently his own house, reared like a small caprice of a palace, at the end of the *Lindenallee*.

Thus exposed to the danger of complacency, a noise, half ribald, half dismayed, seemed to issue out of the professor's nose, and he would be forced to glance back over his shoulder, embarrassed by the possibility that someone had heard, amused to think that someone might have.

In time, and his responsible position, he grew greyer, thicker, deeply scored, until those who watched him on the podium were sometimes less conscious of his words, however subtle and illuminating, than of his rough-hewn, monolithic figure. On his regular walks he took to carrying a stick—it was thought to be an ashplant —for company rather than support, and was always followed by a little, motheaten dog called Teckel, whom he would address at intervals, after turning solemnly round. He dressed usually in a coarse, and if truth were told, rather inferior tweed, but was clothed also in an envelope of something more difficult to assess, protective and provocative at once. Those who passed him would stare, and wonder what it was about the large and ugly Jew. But, of course, there were also many to recognize and greet a person of his standing. Until the decade of discrimination, Germans as well as Jews were pleased to be seen shaking Professor Himmelfarb by the hand, and ladies would colour and show their teeth, no doubt remembering some story of his disreputable youth.

As for his wife, the *Frau Professor* never on any account accompanied him on his walks through the *Wald,* and was only rarely seen strolling with her husband over the red, raked gravel of the park. Her upbringing had not accustomed her to walk, except to the approved shops, where in a light of bronze fish and transparent oils she would celebrate the mysteries of which she was an initiate. In her middle age, she had grown regrettably heavy of body, while preserving a noticeable gaiety of mind. And would lift up many who were cast down. On occasions, for instance, when the women sat and sewed garments for those of them who had been taken too soon, when young girls trembled and pricked their fingers over the *tachriechim,* and older women grew inclined to abuse their memories, it was Reha Himmelfarb who restored their sense of